REMATCH

OTHER BOOKS BY JOAN HAWKINS

Bailey (2012)

Trespass (2013)

Underwater (1974 and 2014)

Family Money (2022)

REMATCH

a novel

Joan Hawkins

Landon Books, New York

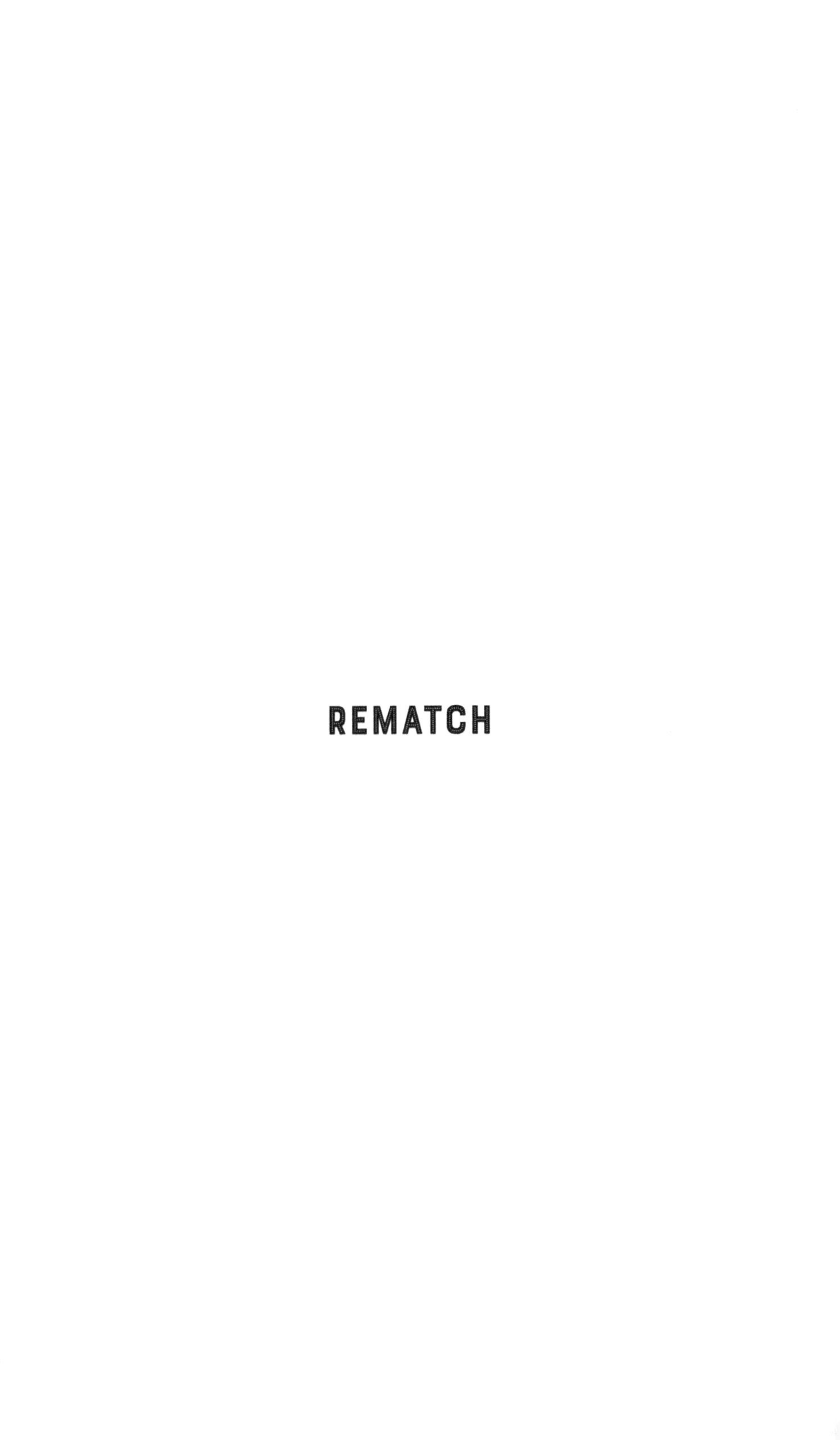

REMATCH

CHAPTER 1

"Mr. Smith!" Her high heels clicked behind him on the marble floor of the lobby as though she'd been violently pushed. Hauling open the heavy glass door, passing the stranger through, Han felt his depression lift like magic. In the dim street he glanced sideways at the wild-haired young woman in a purple jump suit. Her purple shoes darted ahead of her wide cuffs.

"Who are you?"

Her black, densely curly hair bounced on her shoulders as she walked beside him. "I'm one of the unknown multitudes toiling in your law firm. I'm your friendly associate." She slid the zipper of her purple jump suit quickly up and down.

"If you were to ask, I'd tell you that this garment wasn't chosen to protect my health or my reputation. Every day I sport the brightest colors I can buy in the hopes of drawing all eyes." Her wry look disappeared then, and she frowned. "By the way, Judge Smith is your father, right? Well, I think he's a jerk! His decision on abortion was mortifying to women. Of course, we should be the rulers of our own bodies."

"I thought the hand that rocked the cradle ruled the world."

While there had been times when anger at his father had caused Hannibal Smith to mentally call him "a jerk," he had never imagined saying it out loud or hearing such an insult on the lips of others. But here was this rakish girl somehow matching his stride on heels that would do for a call girl and he could not be less insulted or alarmed.

Han paused at the corner and pushed his glasses up his nose. He looked down the street at the subway steps where he expected her to disappear. "When I next see Judge Smith, I'll be sure to tell him that his ruling is controversial."

"It's obnoxious!"

As he turned down Maiden Lane to the harbor, the girl kept by his side. Lightly touching his arm, she pointed back to the subway entrance.

"Why aren't you running for your train?"

"I'm going for a walk in Battery Park." Her presumption continued to amuse him.

"But you'll miss your train to Pleasantville. The boys will be asleep when you get home. The great steak Alison bought will be back in the freezer and you'll have to eat cereal again."

"How can you possibly know so much about my life? Could you be the little face on the window?" Han was warmly incredulous.

The vigorous energy of her gaze and voice, the bounce of her step and her saucy spontaneity seemed unallied with the dark, dreamy face that was always reflected on the office window as he telephoned his wife each afternoon. Reaching for the phone at four o'clock, he had the illusion of being alone in the large conference room because the files stacked up and down the long table formed a wall between the six associates and his desk. But when he'd spin round his chair to look south out the window where his house was buried in the romantic distance ten miles away, the bottom corner of the glass unfailingly reflected two piles of folders carefully parted and a face pushed forward to fill the space between.

"You *are* the face in the window." Han took her hand and shook it. "How do you do. You must be crazed with boredom to listen to all that inane domesticity."

"I like to listen to your conversations. You sound so much in love."

His close view of what for weeks he had sensed, her deep, sweet melancholy, made him want to clasp her shoulders in a protective grip.

"Crazed with boredom, you poor girl."

Again, she ignored his banter and inquired why he wasn't on the six o'clock train to Pleasantville. When he explained that he was treating himself to a brief walk in Battery Park before he went back to work on a memo that must be ready by the following morning, she walked beside him toward the harbor, her head and shoulders drooping.

"That's sad, " she said.

"Oh, awful," he teased her. "Really tragic."

"You guys sure eat a lot of steak."

"As you pointed out, I usually get cereal."

Han's bright laugh didn't influence her mysterious mood.

"When I work late, my wife gets to drink all the wine," he said, then forgot her as he looked about. The sun shone on the tops of the buildings and on the parched trees in the park. Ahead, Han could see stillness. But here, in the narrowness of the ancient downtown thoroughfare, the air speeded up from a pleasant breeze to a wind, as though gaily displaying a physical law. Bits of paper all along the way were lifted up, recklessly spun and abandoned.

"Always a circle." Han pointed at the dash of paper round his knees. "I wonder why?"

"Bitches, out of my way!"

Han started as a sheet of newspaper sailed towards their heads. Ducking, Han saw a stumpy old woman dressed in black. Coming fast, as though stalking a mischievous pet, she rang the cobblestones with a thick, black cane. Han jumped from her path. A muffled moan from the girl made him turn back. The newspaper had wrapped around her head.

"Turn around," he cried, trying to pull the clinging paper from her face.

"Bitches, out of my way!"

The girl rocked slowly from her toes to her heels trying to extricate herself from the newspaper. The old woman bore down.

"Pissing, shitting, farting bitches – OUT OF MY WAY!"

Raising her cane, the old woman thrust it between the girl's legs. She butted her chest with the top of her head and knocked the girl flat out on the cobblestones.

"What's happening? What's going on?" Paralyzed with horror, Han watched the old crone trample over the bright purple body and disappear around the corner.

The girl lay, staring up at the evening sky, struck Han as ludicrous. "You just stood there, then – zap!" Han's raised arm went flat, "she marches over you. I don't believe I saw that. "

"One, two, three, four," she counted slowly. "Four footprints. On my chest."' Her look was full and unresentful.

"Poor girl," he murmured, suddenly sorry. "You were so passive. On your feet, now. Up you come."

"I'm freezing!" She clutched his arm. "I'm so cold." Holding her as he looked about, Han thought it very strange that for the duration of this scene, so bizarre and pathetic, and even now, this well-traveled lane should be as empty as a private driveway. He looked around and saw a sign over a doorway.

"Inn." He read, aloud. A lost word – a command – anything but the name of a pub that he'd never seen before.

Arm in arm, they crossed the cobblestones and went down some steep steps. The blue door had weathered to a pale, shabby hue. As Han pushed the door open a chip of wood drifted onto his sleeve and clung unnoticed among the buttons.

Inside, Han stopped short. It was too dark to see anything, and the smell was intimate and familiar, like a clothes closet. Then someone lightly touched his shoulder.

"Don't go, children. I've got fine drinks here, fresh fish and the best meat in the area. What nice summer suits you downtown people all wear." The voice was rich, deeply accented with inflections whose origins were elusive. Still courteous, the pressure on Han's shoulder increased.

"Glad to finally get one in the place. Day after day, I've watched that gray cotton river flow by. I'll be boarded up before I see the river change to winter wool in all those dark little shades."

They were pulled a few steps forward by a ßstrong grip, the wooden floor creaking beneath their feet. His eyes finally seeing in the dark, Han verified what he'd expected from the voice and spicy smell. A large, fine-boned man.

"Do you mind?" He pulled his wrist from the other's audacious grip.

"It's comfortable. And snug. I built all these booths. I built the bar. Do you like that high sound you hear?" The man's face and dark tunic became clear. The cut of his hair was neat and full, and he wore one unusual earring, which reflected in a glass candle holder nearby. Han's eyes darted away.

"Hear it?" The sight of his powerful chest as the man clasped his hands behind his back made Han try to keep his irritation from showing.

"That's the generator from the subway, but have you ever heard such a *travelling* sound?" He put one hand behind his ear. "I'm fine just listening, but I'm going broke at a thousand miles an hour. I stand by that window watching the gray suits. I rap on the glass. I open the door and let the music rip, but you two are the first in a week. The first since I opened – yes you are – and now I'm going to buy you a drink."

Han's intense pleasure at the thought of a drink was the first familiar feeling since turning down Maiden Lane. The solidity and reason of his normal life returned. He'd order a whiskey, drink it fast, put the girl in a cab and get in a few more hours on the memo. At eight he'd call Allison and tell her to expect him at midnight.

When they were seated, he looked sympathetically at his companion. "Are you in pain?"

The girl's raised shoulders looked like a brace for her head as she sat, very still, in the booth.

"It's your stomach, isn't it?" Han pulled a strip of white tablets from his jacket pocket and handed them across the table. Her suspicion made him laugh. "Antacid, not poison – for your stomach. I chew them all day long." He waved the cellophane strip. "Take two before you drink your whiskey."

As he said the word 'whiskey' Han flashed with happiness and he remembered his mother saying when he was a child, 'don't forget, next week brings vacation.' Han savored this rare excitement even while he forced himself to look the proprietor coldly in the eye to keep him away from the table. Did he think he could hang around just because he'd offered to buy them drinks? Han kept his eyes on him until whoever the hell he was had settled by the window at the other end of the room, looking out.

"It's so strange tonight!" Han's back was martially erect in the booth. The girl didn't hear him. He smiled at her as his fear passed. For an instant as he looked at the big man's reflection on the front window, he'd seen a machine gun slung across his enormous chest. An effect from some shadow, no doubt, but the gun had been so clear to his eyes.

"Better than medicine." The girl clicked her empty glass. She glanced at her wristwatch.

"I hope the feeling lasts while I study. Will you tell me what case I've been working on? Never, ever, have I been so well paid and so bored. Why was I hired to sift through a personnel file eight decades long and separate the applicants to Moss, Poke and Fog by their gender?"

"How long have you been on those files?"

"Last January, at the end of the month I was shoved into that tomb your firm calls an office. The wall to the right of my desk is lined almost to the ceiling with boxes just bulging with forms filled out by women, while to my left," her hands graciously gestured, "meet the men."

"January."

Han counted on his fingers. "That's almost nine months. You must be just about through Phase One."

"And God said, 'rejoice, you have reached the end of Phase One.' Reveal the urgency and excitement of Phase One please. I'm dying to hear."

Han absorbed her ridicule with ease, welcomed it, in fact, as he explained that although somewhat tedious, it was necessary that Phase One be completed so that the more stimulating work of Phase Two could begin.

"I know how you feel." His smile broadened at her stifled stare. "I reviewed documents my entire first year here. It was a nightmare. But you mustn't stop telling yourself that Phase Two will be more interesting. This whole screening process will be narrowed down. You'll see."

"Oh, joy!"

"No. Really." He curbed his barking laugh. "You've got to check the names in the Office Directories against the names you've separated from the applications in the personnel files."

"I can't wait!" She sucked the ice in her empty glass. "I never expected work at a big law firm to be so fascinating. But, please, enlighten me. What are 'the Office Directories'?"

"Well, it's the yearly list, bound and printed, of the names of the partners and associates of the firm. When you are ready to go on to the second half of your labors, the library will be requested to send you up the seventy-five volumes that you'll need to cross check against the boxes stacked along the wall of your dismal room."

With this revelation, her savage mockery transformed her face to handsome effect.

"You know, for the past four years, I've been going to law school at night. I'm in my last quarter. I've been killing myself to become a lawyer – not some dead head clerk."

Han shot up his hand for a second round of drinks. When the

full glass was in front of her she lowered her lips to the rim and took a tiny sip.

"I thought lawyers read cases and wrote briefs. I thought they went to court and argued with each other, but since January I've been like that jerky fairy story girl who had to spin straw into gold. I've never had so much gold," she spat the word out. "I eat out every night because I can afford it and because I'm so desperately bored all day long – spinning that gold – that all I can think about is food,"

"Steak?" Han suggested, "The man said he had good meat. Let's order."

They were both eating vigorously and sharing a bottle of wine when she said she was going to quit before she was ruined by the money. Han painfully gulped his mouthful of steak.

"You're working on a very important case," he gasped, "The implications for this firm – for all the big firms, really – are enormous."

"What case?" Her solid, graceful hand cautioned him. "You must chew meat." She clicked her teeth to show him how. "You nearly choked."

The case will be won or lost at your level. Associates come and go like the wind in this office. If you're still around to work on Phase Two, then Harry Rodman must be impressed with you."

"Before I have to go – Phase Two of what, please."

"When you're finished and we're able to compare the genders of the applicants to the genders of those accepted, this firm is going to come out smelling like a rose." Han lifted her empty glass.

"Can you really go home and study after this?"

"No."

"Let's have another, then." Han turned in the booth and raised his hand. "A nightcap and then out."

"Maybe then you'll tell me."

"Spies use liquor, you know."

"Not the top ones." "

"Law school's a front, then?"

"You'd believe I'm a spy like that!" She grinned and snapped her fingers. "Because I'm a woman. The reason that no one's ever told me what damn case it is I'm working on, the reason that I've been sealed off from the rest of the office, the reason that I'm like the village idiot sent out to collect all the black and pink pebbles I can find on the beach is because, and *only* because – I'm a woman."

"You're paranoid, I'm afraid, but beautiful."

"I'm not beautiful," she reproached him gently.

"Just then you were – when you sounded off. Anger becomes you. " Suddenly, Han was happy. "What's your name?"

"Sylvia Stride."

"That's some cover."

"Sylvia Stride from Seattle, Washington."

With a whoop of laughter, he marched the fingers of both hands across the table.

"It's a ridiculous name, isn't it?" Stalwart and pained, her eyes held his. "Mother isn't exactly subtle, I'm afraid."

"Talk about subtlety. My father named me after the most famous general in the world. Only in an old-fashioned military school could the name 'Hannibal Smith' pass without hilarity.

"I thought your father named you after a Southern ancestor who commanded troops in the Civil War."

"Not only a spy but a frivolous one. Where'd you hear that for god's sake?"

"You're the hero of the associates. Harry Rodman's the toad. The women give you high marks for consideration, humor and good looks while the men admire your brains. We all thank god every day that we don't work directly for Harry Rodman."

"That's very nice." Blushing with pleasure, Han ducked his head. "You're a great group."

"You fell in love with a beautiful, bright society girl in college and married her on the spot. You live in a lovely old farmhouse by a river and have two blond sons. "

"My wife wasn't really a society girl. She was on a total scholarship at college. Her parents were both actors, alcoholics." Han felt strangely compelled to tell her everything. "Gypsies, Alison calls them. They're both dead."

"But she is beautiful and intelligent." The girl's earnest insistence, almost a plea, was unnerving. Would she next seek confirmation on the status of their love?

"How could all this possibly interest you?"

"It's the files, I'm afraid. Sensory deprivation. "I'm in love with success. You're successful."

A vengeful prophecy? An accusation? For the second time that evening, the girl's mournful solemnity was reminding him of his awkward, ribald adolescence. He fixed his eyes on her set features and was relieved that his voice wasn't cracking.

"Why are we being so boring?"

"I was born boring. I was a boring baby. When I was three and went to nursery school, I realized that I was the most boring child in the room. I was a silence freak. I wanted to be mother's favorite child, so I studied all the time. She said life was a horse race. She demanded that all her children be thoroughbreds and for a while we were all neck and neck. Then my older brother flunked out of medical school and became a druggist. The other boy in the family never learned to read and my sisters are on the other side of the Rockies, all married, breeding and praying for thoroughbreds."

"Is that all true?"

"Would Sylvia Stride lie? You look so sympathetic. Why?"

"How depressing, how grim to race."

"Not at all!" She cried, startled. "It's just like you! It's exciting!" Blood rushed into her face as she opened her purse. "I've got to go home and study. I'm paying," she called after Han as he went down the bar to the window.

The proprietor refused to take any money. Folding the two bills, he poked them into Han's breast pocket with such modest and humorous ease that Han felt challenged to prove his earlier assumption that the man had aggressively wanted to sit down with them.

"We came by chance this evening. That girl and I are strangers and we won't be back. Please." Han re-offered the money.

The man's superior height, as he again refused payment, coupled with his persistent humor, struck Han as an insult. He walked back to the table to answer it with one of the bills. Han groaned as the girl also put down money.

"That's the tip," he explained.

"I pay half," she smoothed out the bill.

Han's excitement at her combativeness continued in the bright evening light. The lethargy of digestion always threatened his efficiency, but tonight, walking beside Sylvia to the subway stop, Han was alert. Colors, sounds and smells crowded his senses.

"Don't go back up there," Sylvia pointed to the tower of the building where for fifty years Moss, Poke and Fog had rented three floors for their office,

The contrast of sense and sight absorbed Han. Sylvia's physical presence was vital and assured, but under the loom of the buildings, despite her tall, garish figure, she looked vulnerable.

"Rodman must have his memo." Han smiled at her disgust.

"You could see the sunset from the train if you went home now. The summer air must smell so good in the country. The boys will be on the river. You'll hear crickets." Sylvia's delight became gloom as she looked skyward at the tower where they worked. "How can you bear it up there tonight?"

Han looked up and saw a prison. "You're right. I can't."

"Come on!"

The girl's speedy feet on the steps and the subway's fiesta smell was an unexpected holiday.

CHAPTER 2

Sylvia held out her hand as the subway train pulled into the station. Han intended to bow, but he kissed her instead, his lips barely touching her mouth. He stepped up to the window and touched his fingers to his lips as the car pulled past her. Leaning close to the window for a last look at her, Han was surprised by the sight of his excited face reflected on the glass.

Blushing, Han glanced about the car. With the girl gone, the pleasure of his expanded sensibility became alarm. Sitting beside Sylvia in the station, he'd liked his fellow passengers. Now, his witnessed exposure made him sweat. How dare he kiss her – a stranger? At dinner he'd told her she was beautiful. In her presence a weird spontaneity had stripped him naked.

The memory of the girl being trampled by that horrid old woman in Maiden Lane made his routine passage from the subway to the platform of the Pleasantville train a blind trek. Sylvia's hair spread out on the cobblestones – that bright body trampled – Han shuddered at the images in his head as though that obscene encounter was a sexual mortification he should not have seen.

"What am I doing in this train?" Han frowned at the sunset. Was the girl in the purple jumpsuit the damned Pied Piper? So natural, so easy. A vacation. A girl overtakes me in the lobby. I swing open the door, follow her onto the street and we both go on vacation."

Alison's economy kept the front of the Pleasantville house as dark at night as the ancient evergreen tree that loomed over its roof. Wedded by their absence of light, the house and tree appeared to Han a massive structure of reproach awaiting his return from the city. The oppressive consciousness of some unremembered crime always slowed his step from car to house, but, tonight, the reason for guilt was clear. Symbolizing the pain of consistency, the struggle for permanence, the house and tree condemned his swerve from routine with their dense propriety.

"I'm not supposed to look at sunsets," Han thought as he walked around the house to the back door. The melon next to the ringing telephone on the kitchen table was the same size as the face of that zany associate that daily appeared on his office window. Deft and graceful, Alison hurried to the phone.

A cascade of country sounds followed Han into the kitchen. He heard the whir of a nearby cricket as he started to close the door, then pushed it wide as Alison welcomed him with a wave.

Alison was beautiful. So pert and pleasing as she talked to their neighbor about taking the dog for a month while they went to Europe. Dressed in shorts and a tee shirt, Alison looked at her arms and legs as she talked. Han admired her graceful muscles and her freckles in frank array. When she poked a long cigarette between her lips, she looked like a cocky urchin.

"Unbelievable!" Alison hung up the phone.

"You're so charming." Han wanted to hug her but was forced to step out of her purposeful path as she passed him and shut the kitchen door.

"You just let every mosquito in the county into the house! That was Tinker. George has packed two suitcases, taken the sports car and gone."

"George Hardin? Gone where?"

"Gone to be happy."

"That's incredible."

"To want to be happy?" Alison rummaged in the drawer for a match. "Immature and foolish, I'd say – not incredible. What *is* incredible, in view of all the favors Tinker Hardin's gotten off me, what is – damn it all – truly incredible, is her reneging on the dog."

"Why did George leave Tinker?"

Alison seemed to resent his curiosity. "Tinker says she's barely making it. She's certain that any extra responsibilities will sink her. Well, dearie, join the human race."

"Poor Tinker."

"She deserved it." Han knew that if he criticized his wife's bitter spirit, his anger would be converted to guilt by the storm of her sorrow. The loud message of the passing years was that her life was a tragedy, caused by a college pregnancy and an adolescent marriage. Her scornful rejection of what she called his 'superficial remedies' made him feel not only guilty, but a fool. If he thought that a move to the city, help in the house, a go at a job or a return to school could possibly redress her great disappointment, then Han had no sympathy in him. He would show her more respect if he made her a drink.

"Why does Tinker deserve it?"

"Everyone deserves what they get. I deserve Tinker's ingratitude because I was too trusting to see her selfishness. We're about to leave for Europe and I've still got to line up someone to take the damn dog, someone else who'll renege at the last minute. I can just count on a crisis at the last minute, can't I? Damn it! Where's the matches?"

"You stopped smoking for an entire month." Han put down the drinks on the kitchen table and struck a match. The smell of smoke was exquisite.

"I'm only up to five a day."

Coils of cigarette smoke settled into Alison's short, lively hair. Han sniffed her head like a dog and was happy. Cute and wry, Alison beguiled him as she always had, always would.

"You look great!"

"God knows why after the day I've had."

Her feet tucked under her, elbows on the table, Alison's self-absorption was as childlike as her perky demeanor. A drink and cigarette launched his wife for pleasure.

"Where are the boys?" Han sat down beside her.

"In their cave."

"Why?"

"Today I drove them to the best boys clothing store in the county and bought sports coats for Europe."

"Is that why they're sulking in their cave?"

"They wanted windbreakers." Her empty glass slid across the table and hit his hand. "Don't you dare go out to them, Han. They were dreadful today. A courtroom would be mild compared to the battle I had this afternoon. I need another drink just to tell you about it."

As Han put down her drink and went to the kitchen door to listen for the boys, Alison got up and poured more whiskey in her glass.

"It's so quiet."

"Maybe all their whining and bickering has done them in. It certainly has me. You wouldn't have put up with it for one moment. Oh, no. The boys might be swords of hostility, but you wouldn't care. You'd just go, chop, chop!" Alison clapped her hands, "and the jackets would be bought. I should be as mean as you, but I listen to them. I looked at the windbreakers. I even admired them for what they were. They were perfect for the river, but the month of August will be spent in Europe. Freddy hated me quietly as he always does. But Peter followed me about the store. 'Please, please! The windbreakers could be our Christmas presents.'"

"On the drive home they sat in the back seat where I couldn't get at them. They hated their new jackets. They don't want to go to Europe."

"I hear them." Han lunged past the table. "They're at the front door."

The boys were on the stairs when Han got to the front hall. They stopped on the landing and grinned down at him.

"Freddy just caught the biggest bullfrog."

Peter's hair was too long and his clothes, even for summer, were disgustingly dirty.

"I did, dad. But I let him go." Freddy's knees jutted through the holes in his jeans.

"Your mother tells me you two gave her a hard time today."

Looking at each other, then down at Han, the boys' excitement over the bullfrog blocked their memories.

"We did?" They asked in unison.

"What's the story about the windbreakers?"

"It's some new material, dad, said Peter. "I could hardly feel it. So light and warm. So great for sailing on the river or sleeping out – hey, mother's coughing!'

Concerned by Peter's alarm, Han followed his son to the kitchen.

"You're forbidden to smoke!" Peter plucked the cigarette from Alison's mouth and tossed it on the floor. He went to the sink and filled a glass with water. "You can't smoke cigarettes anymore." Peter pounded her back. "You cough your guts out every time. Look! You can hardly stand."

Peter grabbed Alison round the waist. Bracing himself against her drunken weight, he began to cry. "Cigarettes make her so sick, but she won't stop."

At first Han thought his own tears were an imitation of Peter's. Wiping his eyes, despising his cheap emotion, he was suddenly desperate with pity for Alison as he descended the stairs again to the kitchen. What was the reason for her stubborn sorrow? As a child, as a girl, what had happened to her? Han wanted her to lean on him as well as on Peter. He went over to her, wanting to comfort his wife.

"Poor kid." He stroked her hair.

When Alison raised her head and chilled his heart with her fierce reproach Han bolted from the kitchen. He ran out to the car and stood with his back to the house. Clenched with mortification, waiting for detachment, Han shivered and sighed.

CHAPTER 3

The window of the subway car was filled with the reflections of normal faces and hers was among them. When a passenger got off at a stop, the reflection of the young couple kissing filled up the sudden space. Sylvia leaned towards the picture of mutual desire and from the depths of her intoxication came a song which she silently sang the forty blocks to her station: "I can feel attractive with a man. I can really feel attractive with a man!"

The high spool of subway sound wound her up to joy. At the restaurant tonight, she'd been a perfectly normal person. She'd talked with gestures, even sounded off a bit. Oh, she cherished tonight! Tonight, had put such a rip in her silence that it might never close round her again. She'd been normal, with perhaps even a tilt to colorful, and might she not remain, after the liquor had folded its wings, a newly initiated member of ordinary mankind? From now on, might she not just talk, laugh and listen with the casual confidence that was everywhere in such abundance? Running up the subway steps her vigorous heart disdained the detachment of the moon.

"Here," she thought with every beat. "Here, here. I want to be here."

The horrid cobblestones had jabbed her back, but she'd felt his fingers on her head. His confident touch had drawn out her fear. That hideous woman head butting her – so what. She'd felt attractive with a man.

Hannibal Smith. Han, he was called. His father was a Federal

Court judge. When she'd pushed him to tell her about the case she was so blindly assisting, his wiliness showed that he'd been trained to maintain a ruler's discretion. From birth, she mused, he'd been trained for deceit.

His manner had been so casual – those warm eyes – that even while she knew she was hearing absolutely nothing about the case, she had to struggle to believe it. That kind of craft wasn't learned in a day. Appreciating, as many of her feminist friends would not, that his professional reticence and circumspection were an automatic response to inquiry or challenge, Sylvia's instinct was to imitate, not resent. The young man's play-acting tonight wasn't personal, nor did it mean that the case was important. It simply meant that in the future Hannibal Smith would not be less than a powerful, distinguished man.

What had come over her, dashing to catch him in the lobby? How had she known that her audacity would engage him? From the distance where she'd doted all these months she'd always been frightened by his calm good looks. Her loud heels had rushed her into terrible danger, yet she'd been certain of success.

Sylvia unlocked her door, stepped into the stuffy, narrow space where she lived and immediately fastened the chain. She took off her shoes and pushed her feet through the thick rug to the end of the room. She smelled the paper shade of the Chinese lantern as she flicked the light switch, then laid her hand gently on the worn ribbed paper.

"Insane!" Nervously smiling, Sylvia brushed at the heel prints left on her jump suit. The horror of that backwards fall, its flair of pain had obscured the humor of the scene. BOINGGG! Snorting, giggling, she wiped her eyes.

During her first examination several years ago, the doctor had wanted to know when she had first fallen. Unwillingly she'd told him that it was on her first date. Overriding her intention to like a boy, her body had crashed. Famous for her falls, throughout high school desire dogged her, left her weak and melancholy in its heavy clamp. Hands on her breasts, the heat of a mouth was what she wanted yet she was ashamed to know that outside of her fantasies she had never responded to a boy.

The first week at the huge California college where she'd spent four years, she saw a young woman as tall as herself drift back under a tennis ball and with a quick, deep curve of her back, the racket flashing, take the point. Sylvia stopped dating and learned tennis. Forehands, backhands, serves. The last twenty minutes of the sessions she would practice overheads, her spine springing as she arched and hit, arched and hit.

Sylvia stepped to the window and looked out at the narrow yard while she undressed. After work every evening, Sylvia welcomed the feeling of her bare back and shoulders. Her breasts and stomach, her thin, tough legs raced into her notice like hungry pets. Tonight, she had good news.

Switching on the radio, she went into the bathroom. She jammed her jump suit into the full hamper and filled the sink with water. As she washed the low notes of a current love song vibrated in her chest and for the first time she saw her body as gracious and welcoming.

He had said she was beautiful. "But you're *not* beautiful," she reminded her dark face in the glass. For an instant she saw his face. His calm qualification that anger became her, drew her mouth into a helpless smile. She had felt attractive. That warm, casual way of Hannibal Smith, as though she was his equal. How new, how momentous!

For the first time tonight she'd been thoroughly warmed by male admiration. "I want to race," she said to the memory face behind her own features, so golden and calm. If they sat and drank together a second time, she'd tell him about her mother driving the car past the Orwell Horse Farm, the blue wooden fence that marked its property whipping past the car window as inside, Sylvia listened to the lecture she knew by heart. In the previous century, rich Yankees had come West with the railroad, bought up the mountains and started to mine. They built great houses to live in and fenced off thousands of acres for the horses that they bred and trained to race back East. They also trained their children in institutions there – where culture had flourished for three hundred years.

"You're my thoroughbred," proclaimed her mother with her bitter pride, "out of them all, you're the one who's going to win!"

"I don't have to race," Sylvia would explain to Han with an excitement no less intense than she'd felt on those long-ago days in the car, the hair on her arms and legs prickling.

"I *want* to!"

CHAPTER 4

Hannibal Smith retook his seat at the restaurant table. He'd shot to his feet as Sylvia Stride, the firm's most recently hired associate, walked past their table on her way to the street.

"I've always suspected your chivalry towards women, Smith. Is it a personal quality?" Harry Rodman took his pipe from his mouth and glared at the young man from under his scholar's brow. "Or are you the passive product of your rarefied upbringing? Myself, I'd dump the nosy bitch if I dared. I mean, seriously. We are in deep trouble. Ms. Stride knows about the resumés."

"It's my fault, Harry, I let it past me."

Digging in his pocket, Harry Rodman took out a crumpled sheet of paper, carefully smoothing it before handing it over. The partner growled as he read. "Did she ask you any questions? What did she ask you, Han?"

Han's relief that his confession had gone unnoticed relaxed his jaw and shoulders.

"What she always asks. She'd like to what this case is about. Who could blame her?"

Rodman lowered his eyes to the paper with a look of nausea. "'Law Review:" he quoted. " 'A great pair, but she talks too much.' She knows everything now – that nosy bitch! We're finished."

Recently, Han had become aware that his glasses were no longer enhancing his vision and that he needed a new prescription. His sight didn't go double or blur, but quite often, as was happening now, when looking at Harry Rodman's face, he saw the partner's rigorous, intellectual expression float off his features and hang, distinct but transparent, before a vulgar paranoia.

"You can smile, Smith? Knowing what she knows?"

"Sylvia only knows that we're going to be spending the weekend rechecking the documents for other slip-ups."

Two weeks after a crisis in the sex discrimination case had forced Han to send Alison and the boys to Europe without him, Sylvia had been horrified to hear that the plans Alison had made to have the Pleasantville house painted in their absence had not been changed, so that he'd have to spend several nights in a hotel.

"Hotel?" Sylvia had cried. "That's terrible money! Holy hell, come stay with me!"

The partner held up the Photostat to the small table lamp. Just so, Han had seen Sylvia Stride, squint against the light from their own large office window, studying the smaller print shown in the spaces of the firm's personnel form before she announced that she was looking at a photostat of two documents mistakenly attached when copied. But what was she seeing? *Law review: a great pair, but she talks too much.*

It was an x-ray of his negligence, and Han had shivered as he took it. It was a copy of a female applicant's resume; one of the hundreds of resumés received from graduating law students, personalized by Harry Rodman's lurid, sexist comments in the corner. It had been Han's job to detach these from the firm's own application forms before the latter were produced in court.

"I know she grilled you about the resumés, Smith."

Han denied the accusation with a shake of his head while the word *grilled* coiled him around a sexual memory. She'd challenged him, alright – not only verbally, but physically. Sylvia and he shared their exact height in common and perhaps the same mass, but he'd never expected to feel her strength as equal. Terribly roused, Han couldn't believe that he was suspended above her by those dark, stiff arms and legs.

Chopping at her muscles, then wrestling with her on the thick rug, he couldn't match her wind. She demanded to know what the case was about. Never, ever would he get her to bed until he told her. Christ, she was so strong! Strong, taut and elegant when stripped from the restriction of her clothes. Fresh and fine and springy, every inch a thoroughbred, her mother's pride.

"What?" Han's train of thought returned to the partners' alarm. Rodman's hostility was palpable. "What reason do we have not to trust her, Harry? She's loyal to the firm."

"This case has the most menacing implications for this firm, for the practice of law in this country – even for history, if you think about it."

Again, austere and solid, no face in Han's experience could better express the nobility of arduous thought. It was a face that should be duplicated and sent as masks to all the judges in the country. Criminals would weep before it and who knew, from their tears, repentance distilled.

"But you hired her, Henry." Han spoke cautiously. "You assigned her to the case."

"This is a sex discrimination case. If we're being sued by a woman, we need a woman on our team."

"That's despicable. That's using her." Han stared into his coffee cup. 'That's not fair."

"Do you know what I've come to believe, Smith?" Shifting sideways to the table the partner took his pipe from his mouth and gazed out over the empty tables. "You missed being an associate of Virginia Howe by a year, but when you see her in court, I'm certain you'll agree that she never intended to become a partner in the firm. It's so obvious looking back. She announced that it was 'discriminatory' to make her work in Trusts and Estates.

"Discriminatory?" Han repeated. "We're going to come out of this suit smelling like a rose. We're years ahead of the other firms in hiring women. We were the first to start, we've always hired more, and to prove it we've got the largest Trusts and Estates department downtown, as well as the best. The women are great there."

Turning back to the empty tables, the partner's austere profile pointed Han to the truth. "Biology is a tremendous force, Han. It has to be respected and, not counting Miss Howe, all our women lawyers are deeply relieved to be in a department which both accommodates their particular talents and protects them too. They want to shuttle between maternity and law, and they must if they're going to be stable. The one exception, Han, the only exception, is Virginia Howe. She's not concerned about her rights or money. She's out for something else. For trouble, Han."

Ominously triumphant, Harry Rodman's tone reminded Han of his father's apocalyptic prophecy which had angered and depressed him so many years before. As a result of nuclear ruin, his father had warned, he would probably have no more than thirty years of life to make his mark, a span, he'd joke, that had more than done for his namesake, the greatest military mind the world had ever seen. Hannibal Smith was now thirty-five and ambitious to conquer no less than the trust and admiration of Harry Rodman in the twelve months ahead.

Although still a young partner, Rodman was highly valued for his imagination and blistering attention to detail. He'd been entrusted with some of the firm's most important trials. The sex discrimination case was too uncomplicated for his skill, straightforward, even dull, but extremely sensitive. A woman, having worked for several years as an associate, had been passed over for a partnership. An ordinary event, it was thought by everyone, but not by her. It was her claim that she was better qualified than her more successful male competition and that it was her gender that had caused her to be tossed back into the street. She was suing the firm for a fortune.

"Too bad I didn't fuck off her head," was a typical Rodman snarl. "Her brain's in her ass if she thinks she's better than

Charlie Booth. Smarter than Bill Stuart – where's the bitch coming from?"

Over the previous few weeks, Han had wondered at this odd quirk of his vision that would momentarily expose and dissolve the features of his mentor to expose the bestial face behind.

On the hot street going back to the office, Han looked up at the sky as Harry Rodman's under-face glistened with sneaky prurience.

"August weekend, nobody's around, maybe you can get some."

"Don't be a fool." Briefly catching the partner's eye, Han's tone was indifferent as though he were citing a well known fact. Harry Rodman chuckled and knocked Han's arm.

"It's a break isn't it? Everyone's at the beach and you're in an empty office with your girl associate."

Going into the building Han felt the heat of the partner's loud laugh on his cheek. "Really ... "

"She looks like the type that'll probably do it under the desk. I don't blame you, though. She's a dog."

"What?" Han stopped and faced Rodman in wonderment. "Sylvia Stride is beautiful."

"Oh, boy! You *are* a courtly son of a bitch," he brayed as they entered the lobby of the building.

In the elevator Han looked around at the crowd of lawyers, younger than Harry Rodman but ahead of himself. "Money, manpower," he thought. "Tricky legal tactics. That's not law." Shocked at the words in his mind, Han cast his eyes quickly to the floor as if he'd spoken aloud. "That's Sylvia, " he realized.

"Chivalrous. The very last of your kind." Harry Rodman laughed. "A nearly extinct species. Congress better get on the stick and pass a law to protect you."

Han automatically joined the laughter and felt depression turn him to lead.

As they passed the women's bathroom, the door was swinging shut. The glimpse of the enclosed toilets stayed in his mind and as he urinated alongside Harry Rodman, he longed for the tight privacy of four walls.

"Feel free to use the couch in my office. She's not that bad."

"Who?" Confused, Han slowly realized that "the dog" was the woman he was on the verge of loving. "Sylvia Stride is the best-looking gal in the office."

"What? You don't even want to lay her? No class!" Watching the stream of his urine seemed to soften the partner's mood. "Jesus, Han if you're in this one's corner, I can imagine your gallantry with Virginia Howe. The tits on her," he kissed his fingertips. "That ass! Beautiful!"

"You're disgusting about women," Han declared without heat or humor.

"I'm no gentleman, that's for sure." Cheerful, slightly dreamy, Harry Rodman reminisced about Virginia Howe as he did up his pants."

The first six months in the office she was as docile as little Miss Stride. It was only when she argued that an impression of her prettiness came through. That should have been the tip off. They shouldn't have had to wait for her complaints to realize they were dealing with a spy. She began to wear pants to the office and to chew gum. She used to work with her feet up on the desk and the only man she called "Sir" was the shoeshine boy. When she didn't have on pants, she wore bright, crazy clothes, like a gypsy, and traipsed about on five-inch-high heels. Nevertheless, her work throughout was top notch.

"It's so obvious now." Harry Rodman led the way up the narrow hall. "All she had to do to make partner was act and dress like the other women."

"Was she a spy because she didn't want to go into Trusts and Estates?" Han thought of the ambition of Sylvia Stride.

"Have a nice weekend, Sir Lancelot."

Lethargic, compressing a yawn, Han answered the partner's

mocking wave with a quick salute. He walked down the hall, turned the corner and stopped as the memory of Sylvia's voice filled his mind.

"Holy hell, come stay with me!" She'd exclaimed at Han's news that Alison and the boys had just left for Europe.

"Come hell or high water, I will!" Was his silent acceptance. Aloud, he had demurred.

"I couldn't possibly accept such a favor from you."

"Tit for tat," Sylvia had grinned. "You got me hired."

Indeed, by deleting from his recommendation to Harry Rodman any mention of Sylvia's fighting spirit, Han had ensured her a job at the law firm. Two or three times a week, throughout the fierce heat of July, they'd rotated the expense of dinner at the Inn. Excited by this original woman, the following day Han would assure Harry Rodman that Sylvia Stride was a replication of the only type of female lawyer he could abide – a mental mole, a loyal slave.

Sylvia *was* original. Han supposed it was her western heritage that made democracy, for her, the measure of everything that was good.

Since he'd moved into her apartment, her originality had created a vacation place where his standards and values had been walking on their hands. Learning that Sylvia hated routine housekeeping, it had been so easy just to take over the organization of her tiny household. He'd made up a master list of weekly staples and on Saturday he shopped and pulled the groceries home in a red cart with smooth-running wheels. The only thing Sylvia doted on were high powered cleaning formulas. Cooking didn't thrill her, but when it came to cleaning the kitchen walls, or the shampooing of the thick orange rug, she shimmered with cheerful energy.

When Han first made breakfast, Sylvia would politely tell him that she wanted this or that and inevitably this or that would be cooked and eaten by himself as Sylvia always thought that what he'd put on his own plate was really what she had in mind after all.

"Your egg just looked so much better than mine," she'd ruefully smile. "Gosh, Han, you're a good cook."

Sylvia's predictability made complaint unnecessary. Disregarding her breakfast order, he'd simply duplicate what he wanted to eat himself. It was the same with his sport clothes. On weekends, he soon learned that to wear the shirt and pants that most appealed to him, he must decoy Sylvia and put on his second choice, for the moment she saw him dressed it was that tee shirt and those khakis that she yearned to wear. Having swept into a shirt warm from his back, she'd gloom in front of the bathroom mirror and hate him for looking so much better in his "threads" than she did.

"It looked great on you, it's not fair!" She always said, but he thought her great frown and pointing finger completely adorable.

Coming up to the conference room, Han slid his shoes over the rug. The thick door opened silently. Boxes were piled across the long table like a wall and from the doorway, Han couldn't see if Sylvia was in the room. Was she a dog? Had his involvement made him blind? It was really impossible to remember, but at some point that first evening, in the pub that was now their favorite place, hadn't he recoiled from her appearance? Now the smell of her perfume made him eager and open. He stepped around the table and, slipping his hand into her vigorous hair, he kissed the top of her studious head and dropped into the chair beside her.

"I'm dead with boredom," she said, frowning into the light from the large window. "Your mother called. She expects you to go to the tennis club tonight, with a substitute for Alison."

"The city's an inferno." Han went to the large window, put his foot on the radiator and leaned against his knee. "Why aren't they going to the country? Did mother say?"

"Your father's very tired."

"Mother and her modest expectations! Infuriating! Girls who play good tennis don't stay in the city on an August weekend."

"I play tennis."

Han pressed his cheek to the window. He missed his boys and the river.

"What?" He turned his head. Had she spoken?

"I play tennis."

"This is top club tennis." He followed the shadow of a tern across the harbor.

"Damn it, Han! The class system has ruined you."

Han sat down at the conference table with an affectionate smile. "Another lecture, friends."

"You're no run of the mill snob, Han. Your snobbery is so deep it's physiological. I've changed my mind about that morning at work after our first dinner at the Inn. It was worse than a snub. For a minute you didn't know who I was."

"You can't really think I snubbed you." Han was calm. "You looked so different – a completely different person. You weren't wearing such bright clothes. You were dressed more like other women."

"Not wanting to think of yourself as a snob, you short cut the incriminating process and simply saw me as a stranger."

"That's deep." Propping his cheek on his hand Han looked at the boxes in a daze. "And I'm too depressed to even think about it."

"It is depressing to compromise your wife."

On alert, Han raised his eyes.

"To bring me to your tennis club would be disloyal to Alison and your sons."

"Alison is on vacation and so am I."

"Not me. Oh no." Shaking her finger at him, Sylvia gaily insisted. "I'm travelling fast and far in this elite corporate world. In two weeks, when you go back to Pleasantville, I count on knowing what this case is about."

"Careerist!"

"Absolutely."

Han's hurt feelings changed to arrogance. "You're strong for a woman. But do you really know how to play good tennis?"

"Why do you assume that I don't? There's a gawky geek in your mind, isn't there? Swinging at the ball with spaghetti strokes."

"How did you know?" Han stared at her with hard eyes. "You're right. I do see you as untrained. Can you hit overheads? I usually force a few out of mother."

"Excellent," Sylvia mocked. "You can leave your father to me."

"Ha!" Han pushed back his chair and swung his feet onto the table. "In Dad's day it wasn't done, but if he'd wanted to, he could have turned pro."

"Wasn't done?" She scoffed, but her eyes were interested. She drew her chair close to the table, put up her elbow and supported her cheek as though she was listening to a story. "How old was he then?"

It was one of the things Han found most attractive about Sylvia Stride, that she appeared to be as interested in the past as the present. Not only could he tell Sylvia about his parents' Washington wedding and the presence of the Secretary of State, but his father's war stories were just as well received. She'd listened to the heroic exploits of the youngest Captain in the American Army with shining eyes. The same eyes stayed on his face now as he described his father's remarkable tennis achievements.

"You don't really want to play tennis tonight." He smiled and winked at her sturdy, combative face.

"Yes, I do! I was seeded third on my college team. I'm good!"

"Have you any tennis clothes? What will you wear for dinner?"

"That expression again! I've never gotten used to it and I never will. Quick! Look at yourself in the window. Do you see how you're looking at a stranger?"

On the window of the conference room, in the subway and the streets leading to his parents' club, Han, striving for an objective frame within which to finally judge Sylvia's looks, kept seeking her reflection. Falling back from her quick step, he stared hard at every glassy surface that they passed. It was confusing and unpleasant but her tunic type dress which looked attractive in the black square of the subway windows seemed peculiar, even political, on the glass front of the expensive fish market. For a few instants as she passed, silver fish heads poked out of the vibrant violet sea of her dress and confirmed, with their mournful mouths, that she was a spy.

At the end of the street the club doorman chatted with a chauffeur. As they stepped respectfully out of his way, Han felt himself assume the glacial demeanor of his father. Smiling like his father, he anticipated the judge's amused disdain when he first saw Sylvia. It was amazing that women could learn to walk in those heels. How stoic their vanity! Pushing through the door, Han felt he followed the brazen feet of a whore.

Sylvia stood in the center of the red carpet and turned slowly around as though getting her bearings from the white marble busts that stared with blind eyes from the four corners of the lobby.

"How come a bust of Napoleon?" She poked back her thumb as they walked into the elevator.

"Here, he's kindly remembered as the most successful social climber in history."

As usual, her break-away laugh delighted him, but he became stupidly nervous when the elevator stopped, and they walked towards the locker rooms. Sylvia looked cheerfully around.

"Help! Oh, damn, I left my tennis stuff at James's Street."

"Take off your shoe." Han slipped his foot alongside hers. "Sturdy girl," he laughed. "My stuff stinks a bit – but I can fit you out."

Sylvia peered intently at the plaques that lined the wall, pausing at the name of the victor of the yearly women's singles tennis tournament.

"Mrs. Russell Trowbridge," Sylvia read. "What's her real name?"

"That's a venerable old convention that I'm sure is in use even beyond the Rockies." Han hurried down the hall. "It's called marriage," he called over his shoulder.

When he came back with his cleanest shorts and shirt, Sylvia, was still brooding in front of the plaque.

"It's so weird, Han! She's just disappeared, and in the graveyard, when she finally gets her name back, she'll be known as 'his wife.'"

"Try these," he filled her arms and laughed at her solemnity. "There's no gun at your head, you know. There's *Ms.* and the newly respected Miss and in another decade I have no doubt that every tombstone will read 'her husband.'"

"What if your mother's in the locker room?" Sylvia hung back. "What will I do?"

Han pushed her gently. "She doesn't know who you are."

Alone in the men's locker room, nervously catching a zipper or snapping a lace, Han tried to recapture his optimism. The key was to concentrate. CONCENTRATE! If, for once in his life, he could get himself to really focus on the ball, he would win his father's respect.

"Fuckin' cheap laces." He despaired at the awkwardness and shame that would keep his eye off the ball and leave his arm no better than a stick for feeling.

A tall boy with a tan was standing by the tennis desk. A student, Han decided as he passed. That full hair and relaxed stance – not an athlete – perhaps a dancer. At least his own college days were over. He could give life that much credit.

"First your mother snubs me and now you. Holy hell, isn't this country a democracy?"

"I thought you were a boy." Han held out his hand, astonished. "You look great in my gear. Why are you laughing? I see! You've got your hair pinned up." Studying her as they walked to the court, his spine flashed with heat. "I don't know why, but you've never looked better."

"If I smell, it's not my fault," Sylvia murmured after Judge Smith had briefly touched her outstretched hand and returned to the other side of the court.

"I thought you were kidding, Han, but your mother really wouldn't speak to me. Will she think I'm pushy if I sort of wave now? Hi, there!" Sylvia wiggled her fingers at the still, remote figure on the far side of the net. "She's stayed thin and those cheek bones!"

Han almost tripped over her as she stooped and re-tied the sneakers that he'd loaned her. Brushing the court with her hand, Sylvia stood up with an eager smile. "In California, it's all hard surface – no sliding. This is great!"

As Sylvia went to the back-hand side of the court and set herself to play, Han could see that her flat, one note whistle astonished his parents. He watched his father take a ball from his pocket and start to rally. Rushed and frightened, he could only sense that Sylvia was skilled.

"You're really good, Han! But, I wouldn't hit so hard. Go easy. Make your return real deep. Give yourself a chance to get to the net. Watch." With another light tap on his back, she changed places and swept his father's ferocious shots right back to his feet.

He'd heard this advice before, but never heeded it, at least not playing his father.

"Perfect!" She whispered as he broke his father's service with a hard drive at his feet. "Do it every time."

"Don't lob her, dear!" The judge snapped at his wife as he watched Sylvia drift back under the ball and place it, with a firm grace, two feet behind him.

"It's all mother could do with a shot like that." Han smiled at his father and gestured at Sylvia. "Isn't she great?"

"You must stand at least a foot behind your usual place, my dear. It's an easy bounce if you're in the in the correct position." Judge Smith poked his wife back a foot, but she hit Sylvia's next serve into the net.

"Damn it!" The judge fumed, "will you do exactly as I tell you, dear?"

"She's doing something to the ball," said Mrs. Smith, eyeing Sylvia with sharp suspicion. "She's got something on the ball."

"Sylvia's an excellent player, Mother. Can't you see that?" Laughing, wagging his finger, Han looked to his father for help.

"Shall we discuss this young woman's service after the game? I'd like some exercise." The arrogant swing of his father's hips as he walked back to the line put Han in the grip of a slow burning rage.

"I love you!" Han silently thought, as Sylvia served an ace.

"Keep your position, Han," the judge waved him back to the alley. "That serve was out."

"Dad! It was inside the line! Two inches!" Jutting the handle of his racket over the net, Han pointed at the mark left by the ball. He was still pointing at it when his father flicked his hand at Sylvia.

"Continue, please."

Han skipped back just in time to cover his defensive block. Aiming between his parents, the bounce sailed over their heads.

Sensing his father's frigid rage, Han kept his head down as he walked round the net.

"Do you mind?"

"That was our game, dad. We change sides."

"The score is now deuce."

"What?'

"Get a grip on yourself, boy."

"Dad! Sylvia and I won that last point. The game's over. We won it."

"The score is now deuce, Han. If you don't mind?"

Astonished at his father's behavior, Han hit the ball too hard. He couldn't respond as Sylvia urged him to ease up, and lost point after point. Dashing to the net, his arm tingling from the impact of his return, he saw the judge stagger and take hold of his back.

"You've hurt your father!"

"What happened?" Han grabbed the net, aghast at his mother's venom.

"My fault." The judge waved at Han and slowly picked up his racket. "I took my eye off you. Shouldn't have. You're a powerhouse tonight."

Han's bowels turned to ice at the ancient look of him, the frailty. "What happened, dad?"

"Calm down, Han. You'll get a rematch – you always have."

"But we were way ahead," Sylvia whispered as his parents left the court. "What's he talking about?"

"Han's so competitive." The judge's frosty laugh came through the closing door. "He beats himself."

CHAPTER 5

"Last night at dinner, Sylvia, at one point I looked over at you, and there I was – reflected in your wine glass – this big, yellow dog lying on the table with my nose on my father's hand."

Han's tone this Sunday morning at the office was consistently light and bantering, but wasn't this the tenth time he'd brought up her influence on his vision? Sylvia thrust her hand into the box of application forms to keep her place and looked cautiously across at him. His feet up on the table, he looked at her over the tips of his shoes with a steady, mean gaze.

"Ever since I met you, my eyes have been giving me trouble. I see the wildest things. It's the effect you have on me."

"I suppose that's the first time your father's cheated you."

"He made a mistake."

"I'll say." But Han's calm corrective tone made her whisper.

"It's the effect you have on everything. You change things."

"I didn't make a dent on your father. Every time I asked him about his abortion decision, he'd look at you with that superior, little smile of his, as if I were a monkey. Why shouldn't I ask him about his ruling? Why should that be considered bad taste?" Sylvia's mind went black with rage. "You – are a servile dog. How dare you let him smile that way about me?"

Folding his arms, Han pitched up his chin and considered her as an object, unsightly and superfluous. "You change things."

"Last night you were honest, Han."

"I was drunk."

"But, honest." She glanced at his sarcastic smile, then dropped her head.

Her eyes mechanically returned to the box where her fingers crawled through the mass of application forms that she and Han must recheck over the weekend. At the Inn the previous night, after dinner with his parents, he'd been so fiercely repetitive that she'd given up reminding him that each time the bartender had put down drinks, he'd given the same defense to an accusation that hadn't been made. He hadn't been aiming at his father! He hadn't known where he was on the court. He'd been concentrating on the ball. His father had looked so old!

The bartender's affectionate tolerance, the quick brushing of his big hand across Han's back made Sylvia jealous. He was an imposing figure – mysterious, to boot. He'd managed to side-step any questions relating to his nationality or origins, apart from the fact that he was a doctor, and thus known as "Doc". She felt that a kind of contained lordliness was the mutual attraction between the two men, and with the imposing exile, it made her suspect that the small, always empty pub was a front. Some developing world revolutionary movement could explain Doc's aura of foreign grandeur, but then, more realistically, so would the smuggling of drugs.

The previous night, back in Sylvia's apartment and midway sober from the long subway ride and walk to James's Street, Han had lamented his parents' rudeness and then, his eyes bright stones, he'd swept off his jacket, tossed away his tie and announced that his labor over this extended weekend would be physical as well as mental. Nonplussed, Sylvia had staved off his unrelenting efforts at seduction, determined to use her favours as a bargaining tool.

This summer afternoon, his profile was black against the murky sky in the office window. "I was so near, last night," he said, slightly smiling, although his face was turning hard. "But you must have gotten your hands on one of your potions in the kitchen."

"Oh, so now I'm a witch?"

"Today, though," he reached for the ringing phone, "you're up sixty stories without your magic powders."

Then the phone rang. Sylvia scowled at him for taking his feet off the table, for sitting straight and looking alert simply because his mother was on the other end of the line. She tried to stare him into looking at her so that she could silently mock him. The few times that Mrs. Smith had called before, Han's respectful voice and bearing had seemed to link a distinguished, gracious woman to the conference room; a woman that for as long as Han held the receiver to his ear, revitalized Sylvia with her imagined affection and approval. When plans for dinner were made, Sylvia dreamed it was she, not Han, who would walk on a summer evening through streets of brownstones where children played, and trees grew. Walking among costly smells and sounds, climbing stone steps to an ornate door, it was a ritual of hope.

Even his frown looked respectful, as Han listened to his mother's problems and complaints.

"The entire country has a pain in its back, mother. It's the price of American civilization. Automobiles and gluttony."

With Han at the other side of the conference table, the distance between them seemed to grow as the conversation went on. Sylvia's daydream turned to anger, which applauded her pain as punishment for romanticizing Han's parents. For being stupid enough to be in love with his looks.

She adored everything that chance and money had given him – his voice, for instance, that quite apart from what he said, fashioned romance with its cultivated sound. Hooked on his looks and the sound of his voice (she even loved his smell for crying out loud!). She'd become a nostalgic idiot and deserved being treated like mud by shallow, edgy people, who, for all their money, were hicks. Was he also? Was Han just a hick – like them? Like herself?

Mechanically, she'd plucked out a document and held it up to the office window. Now, her eyes sharpened with his interest as she heard him abruptly end the conversation with his mother and hang up the phone.

"Best legs of the month," she slowly read aloud. 'Excellent record, but I felt she was interviewing me.'"

Han stood and held out his hand.

"Oh, sit down," she murmured as she checked the exposed print. "So, so, so. This hot summer weekend has been sacrificed for a purpose."

Sylvia had found a second document with an oddly unprofessional note in the top corner, and here and there down the page, between the lines, was the kind of show-through that she'd seen before. Smaller print from a different typewriter, but much fainter as if there'd been interference – it wasn't supposed to have been put in the copying machine. It was a mistake!

The fainter print had been typed by the applicant; Sylvia strained her eyes to read it, making out the name of Elizabeth Dubois, who graduated fourth in her class at Virginia Law School.

"You guys are suppressing evidence."

Indulgent suddenly, a fond teacher or brother, Han stood and shoved his hands in his pockets.

"Sylvia," he softly said. "You went to an excellent law school."

"First time I've heard that," she braced. "So what?"

"You should have learned that the top-flight firms in this country do not suppress evidence. If it were discovered that any lawyer had, the guy's career would be over in a second. He'd be a pariah, an untouchable. You should really appreciate the naïveté of that remark. It's completely cynical, which you aren't. You should know better."

"I don't know beans," she yelled, struggling against shame. "But I know that if the case is too sensitive for an associate to know about – me, for instance –" she jabbed her chest with her thumb, "why should I assume that your deceit and wiliness cut off at a certain line. *That's* naive, if you ask me."

"Do you think I'm wily and deceitful?" Han was amazed, "You don't believe that. Not really. You can't."

"I thought you were proud of it – all of you, all the firms." His surprise confused her. "I'm talking about all the tactics you've described. You told me that Harry Rodman could out-rationalize Aquinas."

"Sylvia – think of the boredom! The crushing hours! I'd be dying if I didn't believe in the case."

"I know you believe in winning it."

"Don't you mind working for a shady outfit?" He hated her. "I would."

"I'm going to be a litigator," she beseeched him. "It's the chance of a lifetime to work for Harry Rodman."

With his clipped hair, bony face and severe dark suit, Han reminded her of the prized toy of her childhood, her boy soldier doll.

"You really think we're dishonest? Han shrugged at the murky window. "She thinks Harry Rodman would suppress evidence. She thinks I would."

"Don't call me 'she'." Sylvia broke down. "I'm not one of your initiated. You know I'm too ignorant to know what to think."

He sprang round the table and pulled her from the chair in an unlikely embrace. "You don't feel like a careerist," he whispered.

"You don't smell like a Rodman." Sniffing his skin and hair, she groaned and laughed. "It's primitive to be so influenced by the nose." That sudden hardness of his filled her with a tense dread. "Why don't you tell me what this case is about? I want to be with you so badly."

"It's 2 am and we're leaving." Pulling her to the door, he laughed as she looked wildly around the choked conference room.

"There's so much to do," she said, " We'll only have to come back. Why not stay here? What about Harry Rodman's office?"

"What? You're incredible. No way!"

"What's the matter? Is he there? Why go all the way up to my apartment for a wrestling match? You'll never win."

But the quick thrust of his fist between her legs and his passionate disgust at her pragmatism made her yield. They took a cab.

"This is a case of sex discrimination," she said, as street after street passed, but not the feeling of his indignant fist. Legs of lead lifted her from the cab and walked her to the apartment door. The click of the key in the lock turned her desire into a cramp that bent her over. Like an old woman, she crossed the kitchen and the thick living room rug and dropped on the couch.

"Will you hurry up?" She snapped. "Forget the ice! Holy hell!"

Han came out of the kitchen drinking from a liquor bottle.

"You're the best-looking man I ever saw!"

Sylvia crooned his praises while he took off his jacket and tie. He put the bottle down on the rug and leaned back against the cushion. His cheerful affection drew her like a magnet. When she climbed onto him he swung his legs up onto the couch and held her in a vise, but his lips were subtle. She licked up the moisture of his mouth and sucked on his tongue. She adored bringing her mouth to his and did it again and again.

"It's a sex discrimination case and what we're doing now is getting those see-through photostats out of the evidence before we present it in Court." She loved his temples edged with bright hair. "I saw those Greek statues at the museum once and you look just like them. You're classic and lovely and you've got to tell me why what we're doing is not suppressing evidence."

"It's old-fashioned to use sex as a weapon, you know."

"But I'm in an old-fashioned world – Moss, Poke and Fog." She pressed against him. Plucking out her shirt, everywhere Han touched her, his respectful hands imparted a feeling of beauty.

"Why did I have to spend six months putting all the applications that this firm has received for the past seventy-five years into one box for men and one box for women?"

"Like I said, so that we can easily compare them with the lists of names in the Office Directory."

"Why is it that you make me feel so attractive?" The intensity of her confusion parted his lips as she kissed him. "In the past month I've never once felt you liked me for the wrong reasons. I've never felt beautiful before and you never, never put me down, but I still don't know what the case is about. I'm still treated like a spy – by you!" She said. "Whom I adore."

"Still?" He frowned. "The evidence suppressor?"

"Once, all the application forms were attached to the resumés." She held him off with stiff arms. "Before you had the files copied to comply with the subpoena, the resumés were stripped out because, those, those – "

"Personal comments? What lovely muscles!" He stroked her arms.

"Those *sexist* comments – *a great pair, but she talks too much* – ruin your defense."

"I hate the way you see me, Sylvia!" He pushed her off him. "What the hell are we doing together?"

"Once upon a time there was a young woman who wanted to be a litigator. When she was hired by a famous Wall Street firm and put to work on a case, she was so thrilled that months passed before she realized that she wasn't trusted. Because her law school record was good, and she was conscientious, she could think of no particular reason. Over the years working on Wall Street as a young litigator, she never added one word to a brief, never discussed the case with other associates on the team – god forbid she should talk to a partner. She never, when she finally thought about it, got out of the files."

"When she was finally passed over for a partnership, it was more self-hatred than anger at the injustice of it that made her sue the firm. What got her up for a legal attack was the fact that she could have been so stupid, so blinded by ambition – that she could have tolerated such a run-around and spent such energy hoping that it wasn't what it was."

"You *could* try a case," Han said. "The feminist magazines would love your little fairy tale if it read as well as it sounds. Selfish manipulation, hostile chauvinism, the suppression of evidence, I think it would sell very well."

"If things aren't as they appear, how would I know?" Sylvia pounded the cushion between them. "You got me hired and I want to trust you, but how can I help but see why we're working on this sacred summer weekend? Could I not notice your face when I fished up that second sexist comment? I'm so glad I can hold you off! It's my only pride. MOTHER!" She yelled, to her total embarrassment. She covered with a gay laugh as Han looked wildly behind him.

"I just remembered your message," Sylvia explained. "I've got to call her back." She responded to Han's sympathy with an eager smile. His assumption that her 'problems with her mother' could be added, like his own, to the storehouse of the world's sarcasm on the subject, made her gay with relief. Her mother's dogged, passionate presence in her mind, the voice that was always talking, was in no way diminished by the three thousand separating miles.

"Who are you?" Her mother had asked Han when, at six o'clock the previous evening he'd picked up the phone. Han could only nervously laugh at the memory of the hostility pouring from the receiver into his ear.

"Sure, all this separation of the files and the comparison with the Office Directory are going to prove that Moss Poke and Fog has hired more than its share of women," she tapped Han's knee, "but the sexist comments show that the women who were seen as dynamic were not hired or were never made partners."

"You really are beautiful!" Han said, trying to change the subject. "Is your mother beautiful, too?"

"My mother doesn't give a damn about her looks. 'Looks make you a commodity' is one of her favourite sayings. She must have cared when she was a girl, but last year when one of her breasts was removed because of cancer she said she was glad it was gone. Sinking down beside Han, Sylvia sputtered, "That's unimaginable to me! Oh, god! It really is!"

"You look so guilty!"

"It's her severity." She pressed her face into his shoulder. "That never lets up. She loathes physical pleasure."

"Even sex?"

"Sex never was a pleasure to her. Damn it! If she wasn't always clear about that, it never snows in the Rockies."

"Do you care?" Han was sweetly sincere. "About sex?"

"You know I do!"

"You're in control, then."

Sylvia didn't understand his teasing tone. Did he think she was cold? With some dread, she glanced quickly to meet the confusion her awkward resistance brought forth in men. Her heart thumped with fear. But she could see from his eyes that she was desirable. Springing onto his lap, she gripped his shoulders.

"Harry Rodman and you have a strategy to keep the sexist comments out of sight. You'll bust your brains to find some distinction – is that the word you use?"

"Rationale," he murmured against her neck.

"Because the 'sexist comments' don't reflect facts, like someone's gender, but only casual opinions? Is that it? Is that the rationale you're using? That the subpoena didn't call for personal stuff?"

"See?" His rosy face was triumphant. "Not clever legal tricks but sound analysis." He pulled her down on the couch. "Looking through form to substance, you know, is the crux of the law."

"I do see!"

They sat side by side on the couch and took off their clothes.

Laughing at her neat pile of dress, stockings and underwear, Han tossed his shorts behind him. All the heat in her body escaped as Sylvia let herself be pulled off the couch and onto the thick rug. She smiled up at Han, her arms and ankles convulsively crossed.

But Han understood her resistance as flirtation and with a shocking strength and skill he unlocked her in a moment.

The sex of her fantasies was filled with more sensual substance, heat and motion, and had nothing to do with the shock of this drastic exposure and sudden burst of frantic shame. The struggle to lift her shoulders from the rug exhausted her and when she fell back Han's lordly exertion was an exposure more galling than ever.

"I hate this!" Sylvia howled in her silence. Her fists hung over Han's head and she yearned to cover his back with bruises as he beat against her. At his every inward stroke she read the announcement on the ceiling. She was not a valid person.

"I loved it. Really! It's the relief," she wept at his imperious finish. Hiding from his surprised eyes, she kissed his face and neck until he sat back between her legs. Lightly fondling her breasts, he slipped his hand into the notch of her legs and withdrew it, aghast.

"You've got your period," he murmured. "You're sensitive now. Why didn't you tell me?"

"But I'm not due yet."

Absently transferring the stickiness from his fingers to his leg, Han went pale. "Not due? But, then – oh, no! It's your first time. Is it?" He clutched her arms in dismay. "You tried to stop me. I didn't think you meant it. Oh, poor girl – why didn't you tell me? Why were you so quiet?"

Quietness was the mode of her shame.

"Now I understand all the wrestling. Where are my shorts?" He dashed to the corner and turning his back, whipped the blue cotton up one leg and then the other. He went to the dresser and urgently unstuck the drawer, tossing her one of his shirts.

"This is awful," he murmured. "This stinks to hell – but

I should have known." He glared at his blood-spotted hand. "Virginal strength. The power and the glory!"

"Oh, stop! I'm a contemporary woman. I'd be ashamed not to use sex to advance my career. You got to home base when you finally told me about the case."

"Be accurate, Sylvia. I didn't tell you about the case. You finally put it together."

"You didn't say I wasn't right. Am I right? I'll get you back if you tricked me."

"There's no need to get me back. Somehow, I've got to repay you. This is awful!"

In a fit of hurt, she suddenly shouted, "If I don't care about my damned virginity, why should you?" Her legs moved docilely as he tugged her to the couch. "Nothing's different now! Nothing whatsoever." She accepted his contrite kisses, then pushed him away and set her own cheeks ablaze with two vicious slaps. Han grabbed her hands, his eyes reproachful, filling with tears.

"You hit yourself so hard. I hate your mother. How have you survived?"

"I deserve my mother for some reason."

Han remembered his violent guilt at hitting his father with a tennis ball. "It's like we've both been taken hostage – for some reason."

"For some reason!"

Laughing, they stood and hugged each other hard.

"We should write a book!" Han said.

"Why?"

"In honor of your virginity."

"I'm not interested in my virginity and marriage."

Sylvia was surprised at the calm gravity of her tone while her heart reeled with joy. *In honor of your virginity*, he'd said.

Her virginity had startled him. Not only did he believe in the conventions of his lordly class, but he adhered to them. If it was impossible to exchange a woman's virginity with marriage in the whirl of these new days, then, at the very least, a woman should be honored.

CHAPTER 6

"We've got to go back to work, Han." Sylvia slipped her arm through his as they stood looking in the window of the medical store.

Han bade her look at the bizarre mixture of images in the store window, the jumble of inside and outside, of trusses and buses, of bed pans, wheel chairs and passers-by. Groaning, she tugged his relaxed arm. They were a few blocks above Wall Street at five in the afternoon and all she could see was the looming tower of Moss Poke and Fog, dark and massive, like their neglected work.

As they passed the stone church and turned down Wall Street, Han pulled her back to him and put his arm around her shoulders. "I bet Alison's fallen in love with a French count. I can just see the letter in the post box now."

"Walk faster, Han. I'm going to stall." His arm and body were a prison that her gaze fled. Down the narrow street a taxi stopped in front of the building where they worked. A small, energetic woman stepped smiling onto the curb. Her gray dress adhered to her strong body with a feathery simplicity. She pulled avidly on a cigarette. Han released Sylvia's shoulder hurriedly.

"You're in Europe!" Han greeted the woman with a social voice and smile, but nausea clouded his eyes. "I mean, aren't you in Europe?"

The woman approached. Evidently, Alison was not in Europe.

"I know you!" She took Sylvia's hand and shook it as she coughed.

"You're not supposed to smoke." Han plucked the cigarette from his wife's mouth and flung it into the street.

"A waste," Alison gasped. Her hand in Sylvia's was wet with sweat. "You're the young associate who plays such good tennis. Han's mother told me about you."

Han's constant smile was terrible. As Alison coughed, he dug a handkerchief from his pocket and pressed it into her hand. When it fluttered to the pavement, he bent to retrieve it, but then, groaning, turned away and headed off down the block.

"How absurd." Alison looked after him with a stunned smile. "He's running away!" Han dashed towards the dark church and disappeared around the corner.

"Why aren't I in Europe!" Alison stepped away from Sylvia and dug in her purse. "I've *got* to have a cigarette."

Without warning, she began to sob and softly patted Sylvia's cheek. "Mustn't cry. Can't! God damn it!" Sylvia stared at Alison from the corner of her eye, feeling ruthlessly detached from the woman's distress. Her dress was gray, also her shoes and purse. Against her elegant economy of color and style, Sylvia hated the vivid commotion of her own dress, bag and sandals. Alison's bracelets jangled as she struck a match.

"I know you, tennis player." Blowing smoke from her tense lips, Alison looked frankly into Sylvia's face. "I'm inviting you for a drink. Now, where?" Her darting gaze fixed on the street sign behind them. "Maiden Lane? Well, ho! That's morbid enough for the occasion, don't you think?"

"I've got so much to do."

"Nonsense." Queenly, humorous, Alison slipped her arm through Sylvia's and walked her down the street. Caught off guard by Alison's insistence, she was surprised at her physical hurry while her mind shouted *Run away!*

"I haven't eaten yet, have you?" Alison said, as they came up to the blue door of the Inn. She reached past Sylvia, opened the door and pushed her into the restaurant. "Small, snug and very well done. Good day, sir."

Alison's warm cordiality delighted Doc. He swept up from the dim rear of the bar, his robe in stately flow when he stopped before her.

"One celebratory drink is all we want – if there is such a thing as only one drink. Alison winked at Sylvia. "Could we sit in that splendid booth?"

His hands clasped against his chest, his head bent, Doc's admiration enveloped Alison as it had Han. The circumstance of her appearance with Sylvia in his bar, the details of her life, were apparently of no importance – mere transient bubbles in the flow of his admiration. Who or what Doc greeted in Alison and Han Sylvia didn't know, but her usual disappointment at his indifference to her was now relief as he graciously guided them to a booth.

Alison offered her cigarettes to Sylvia and Doc. "No? Neither of you? Well, bravo!" A dowager's robust approval. "I suppose this high will turn into depression and I'll be eating every minute and crashing about drunk like all my friends who've been left with the kids and a stinking monthly allowance." Alison touched Sylvia's glass with her own and drained it. Doc immediately brought her another.

"Well, cheers my dear. It makes you anxious to sit so long. You're worried about your work because you're ambitious." Alison smiled triumphantly as Sylvia admitted her desire to rise to the top of the Wall Street world. "That's perfect. A litigator. You look smart but honest. You're tall enough and your beauty is earthy and appealing. Juries will like you. They'll know immediately that you're honorable. My ex-husband is no fool to love you. A professional goal in life makes a woman doubly exciting. I can certainly see you two side by side in court."

Sylvia looked up at Doc. Surely, his discovery of Han's betrayal would cause him to condemn the young man he so delighted in. But she only saw admiration for Alison in his half-closed eyes as he set down another drink.

"Hey, lawyer! You're not drinking. You don't join me in my celebration? Quite proper! You have work to do. Then I must feed you. Meat!" Alison tugged on Doc's sleeve. "What meat can you serve my young adventurous friend?"

With a bow, his hands clasped to his chest, Doc explained that his Japanese cook had called in sick.

"Empty place. Japanese cook. This place is a cover for you." Alison shook her finger at him then opened her bag. "You're involved in spying or in drugs. I'd best pay up before you get busted."

Doc plucked up the bill between two fingers and dropped it into her purse. "Please, allow me. You have brought my place luck." Alison grimaced as she snapped her purse. "I bet you're an exiled foreign statesman."

"This booth, the paneling, the bar," Doc's hand brushed Alison's shoulder as he gestured. "I built it all."

"With your own hands?" Alison matched his broad smile. "Let me see."

Alison stood and bent her head over his out-thrust hands. She traced his palms with her fingers and looked around her with respect.

"You do beautiful work. I wish there was near your equal in Pleasantville. My god, what a month of neglect can do to an old farm house."

"Come back!" Doc leaned out into Maiden Lane as they left.

"Never!" Alison turned and saluted him. "Gone, gone, gone! Yet I love your blue door."

For all she had drunk on an empty stomach, Alison's pace was fast and steady. At the corner of Maiden Lane, she tucked Sylvia's arm into hers and looked up and down Wall Street. Hadn't she seen a man selling hot dogs right on that corner? Shading her eyes, Alison pointed into the setting sun. Ah, there he was in front of the church.

Their backs to the sun as they walked, Sylvia watched their shadows as Alison recounted her shock at coming home from Europe a week early and finding the mail three feet high and the house airless as a tomb. She'd telephoned Han's mother and heard about the associate who played such good tennis. When she'd seen Han and Sylvia walking like comrades, she knew the cause of her exploded marriage.

Alison's palpable pain struck Sylvia with the force of a spell. Unable to speak, she stopped on the pavement.

"You mustn't feel badly, Sylvia. You're a product of these times. How could Han resist you? I couldn't if I were him. I wouldn't." Alison stopped to face her. Pressing Sylvia's shoulders and then her cheeks with her confident hands, she triumphantly intoned.

"You're the splendid product of these times."

Alison teased the sullen hot dog vendor. "We can't let this woman go hungry into battle. Give us two franks with plenty of onions and mustard."

Her hands full of hot dogs Alison led Sylvia to the churchyard wall. "I'm no philosopher but I know that to fight you must eat." Sylvia obediently chewed and Alison put another hot dog into her free hand.

"I've drunk my supper, so you dine with abandon. You're the same height as Han. He weighs a hundred and forty-five and I bet you're a good fifteen pounds lighter. But that doesn't matter," she tapped her temple. "It's what's up here that counts. Even physically it's of no matter — for there's always a gun. Maybe I should get a gun. But it doesn't satisfy. No apologies, no repentance. It's all self-pity now and lawyers and insanity. Who isn't insane, underneath and always? Good god, what a struggle for control. Look at Han.

I've never known a person more insistent on self-control." Alison put her arm over Sylvia's shoulder and briefly pressed her finger tips against her working jaw.

"I met Han in college, I got pregnant, we got married and that was that. I was nineteen, a decade ago, but women are so different now, vastly different. I see it in their size and the way they walk and what ambition! I love your hunger. One down and one to go. I bet you could wolf down a dozen. God, I love it. You're a match for men, damn it." Pressing her head to Sylvia's, Alison rocked them on the stone wall. She crooned curses against men in the tone of love.

"God damn his black heart. The tree man says the evergreen will go down in the next storm. But hell!" She hugged Sylvia hard and let her go. "My handsome husband, my bonny bitch of an ex is gone. As you'll be gone in five minutes. Gone, gone, completely gone!"

"It serves me right! It's just what I deserve!" Sylvia whispered as Han's wife pushed off from the stone wall and began to walk away. At the click of the streetlight turning green Sylvia flung into a gallop. Her lungs ached and people wrenched around at the pounding sound of her feet.

"What is this?" A woman yelled.

"God damn my dumb slave's soul. I asked for it."

The financial street was named for the wall the early farmers had built at their backs to protect them from native communities. The setting sun laid down tree shadows on a flight of stone steps. A statue of some historic figure stood at the top, his back to a row of massive columns. Young men stretched their legs in the sun.

"It's too hot to race!" One called as Sylvia ran by.

"I want to." She smiled and struggled to push open the massive glass doors of her office building. "I'm going to."

Shooting skyward, Sylvia remembered voice of that elegant, humorous woman, the voice of Han's wife, merged with the electricity in the elevator cables. In the fast climb up the tower, she was glad that Alison was gone so she could begin to remember her. Alison had been masterful in her shock, unbelievably brave! Sylvia welcomed Han's immediate departure from her life, the chance it would give her to match the nobility of his marvelous wife.

61

CHAPTER 7

Han stared at the street sign. Never much of a runner and currently out of shape, he'd just run thirty blocks without pain or effort. Thirty blocks? Han pressed his palm against his chest. Feeling the furious pace of his heart, he suddenly heard his raucous lungs. For all he knew, he'd covered the miles by reflex in one gigantic leap of dread. He touched his lips. And he was smiling!

The building tops intercepted the red September sun and the reflections on the glass store windows grew brighter as Han walked uptown. A window with a black velvet backdrop stopped him. He faced two female manikins dressed in tweed suits and looked at his reflection in horror. "What the hell am I doing smiling? Stop smiling." With a groan, he stared incredulously at his stubborn smile.

A blue bus barged into the window world. Han ran to the curb and got on. Packed among riders he covered his irrepressibly smiling face with his hand.

Alison's sudden presence on Wall Street had destroyed Sylvia's affection for him. Beautiful, frank, bold yet vulnerable, Alison had confirmed Sylvia's picture of her. If he indulged in vacation flings when he was married to a woman like Alison, then – he'd seen it in Sylvia's eyes – he must be a callow asshole. Dreading Sylvia's condemnation as Alison coughed, Han had fled.

If Alison wouldn't quit smoking, he must insist that she go to a clinic. Most of all, he would have to see that the boys had clothes and baths and stopped looking so utterly neglected.

Quickly walking from the bus stop to Sylvia's apartment, Han decided that if she was still working at the office, he'd pack up his stuff and clear out before she came home. If she respected nothing else about him, she might approve of his alacrity.

On summer nights, up and down the street, doors were open. Deep inside the vast Catholic church, candles were glimmering, and in the grocery store the proprietor rang up his orders with his shrill voiced parrot riding on his shoulder. As Han slowed down, the smell of cats and oranges hung over him like a tree. Bouncing off a car, a yellow tennis ball looped over his head and two old men with thrusting necks and the pace of turtles blocked the sidewalk.

Sylvia would have swerved down this very street to get home. Although Sylvia always rushed like hell, it was she who'd alerted him to his dead nose. Always turning her quizzical face into the breeze, she wondered what this or that smell could possibly be.

Han rapped the top of the newel post, remembering that she'd bent over and sniffed it that morning with a happy sigh. On the bus she'd sat with his briefcase on her lap, her nose drifting along the handle. Wood, leather and cotton were the more conventional sources of her delight, but she also admitted partiality to smells that commonly excite repulsion and are never mentioned except by brazen children. She explained her liking for garbage, excrement and urine as a natural compensation for the sterility of western skies where for almost two decades she'd smelled nothing in the air at all. The nights they played tennis, she remarked on the good smell of his gear, and she liked to wear his shirts when his sweat was in them. For the first time in his life, he'd been informed that he had, in his hair, breath and the various regions of his body, a particular and wonderful smell.

Squeezed together on the couch, lying in the dark, he'd tucked the casual compliment away and gone to sleep. In the morning he'd woken to the joyful memory of her words. Like the breath of the ocean or the land, his unnumbered chemical doings sent up a smell that was liked. Vividly relieved, Han had felt the grace of normalcy.

If he was the first one in at night, it was his habit to take off his shoes in the dark and slide his feet over the rug to silently greet the tall, narrow window set crookedly in the living room wall. The rugged trees surrounding the fierce rock in the courtyard, with the skyscrapers rushing up behind the brownstones – it was his favorite view in the city. The stark room behind him – one couch, one table, one chair and one Japanese print on the white wall – was its unique access.

"I've been having fun!" Leaning into the courtyard, his astonished voice bounced back at him. "I've been happy!"

In the shock of leaving, he'd finally put his finger on why he'd felt that living with Sylvia was somehow free of the hook of consequences. When he'd wondered why his nightly return to this tiny, meager apartment did not depress him, how could he have failed to realize that he was truly in love?

Han pulled a drumstick from the chicken he'd cooked the previous night and turned to admire the bottle of scotch set out on Sylvia's bathtub. No whiskey company in the world would try to advertise its wares using an old-fashioned bathtub standing on four paws and covered with a board to carry the bottle. Yet he found the setting both cozy and stylish. Perched on the edge of the sink, drinking from the bottle, Han remembered that his family's summerhouse had a bathtub that stood on four friendly paws. He lurched as he got up to put away the chicken, and had to cling to the refrigerator door.

Han missed his childhood summers, and he missed the routine of his weeks with Sylvia. Cold and hollow, he didn't want to go back to winters, rivalry and the sarcastic life.

The bright frying pan hanging on the kitchen wall caught his image as he passed it. His horrible smile was gone, thank god, and now the reflection represented a type: stoical, responsible and overworked, a type that stepped out of vacation with a pocket of photos and mild regret and immediately forgot that he'd ever been away. Han felt outraged to see the orange rug whirling under his gaze. Liquor had never done such a job before. He was so dizzy and weak!

"Will you kindly get a grip on yourself?" His father's icy voice rang in his ears. "If you don't learn to control yourself, you'll never amount to a damn."

Holding the arm of the couch, Han gazed at the closet as if it were a mile away. First, get his suitcase down; second, pack up his clothes and third, get the hell out!

"Fool!" Savagely he punched his errant legs. The flimsy closet door jumped on its hinges as he crashed against it. Steadily cursing himself, he slid the door to the side and fell among Sylvia's clothes. Her smell of resin and smoke, the smell of his intimacy, was strong in the bright layers of materials, almost making him weep. Clutching her clothes, burying his face, he felt he was falling off a roof. The vacation was over. As his knees hit Sylvia's shoes, another suck of gravity made him violently nauseous.

"I'm so drunk!" He slapped his hand across his mouth to check the vomit. In a nightmare of numb movement, he got himself into the bathroom and emptied his stomach. He couldn't stop retching and was expecting the next dry heave to kill him, when he felt Sylvia's hands on his shoulders.

"I was so shocked when you ran away. Now I understand. You must have a virus." Han responded to her concern with joy. Could she hate him and still give him an alibi, absurd as it was?

"Why am I so sick, just when I need to leave?" He clung to her.

"You' re not going anywhere."

It was impossible to move out tonight. He'd call Alison and tell her to expect him in the morning. The end was tomorrow morning. But tonight was now and a night, living as they lived, on the spine of the present, was a lifetime.

CHAPTER 8

"Here, Han! I'm back here!" His panic while he hunted for Sylvia in the crowd must have been awful to see, but, really, they had so much to do. Good! He felt his face grow hard as he struggled towards her.

"Why are you standing here? This isn't the right store. Come on!" He gripped her shoulder.

"I want that dress." Sylvia clicked the heavy glass with her fingernail. "That's exactly the dress I want."

Han frowned as he looked in the window. "These reflections make everything so confusing. The manikin in the gray dress is stepping right through you. "

"That's the dress I want."

"Oh, dear!" Han shaded his eyes and peered at the chaste, woolen dress. "That's what Alison would wear to court."

"Exactly!"

In her dread that the last size that would fit her was being sold at that very moment, Sylvia pulled loose from Han and dashed across the main floor of the fashionable store.

"We're wasting time," Han grumbled as a saleswoman bore down. "Strong colors, casual style – that's what you look best in."

"Not for court."

"Especially for court."

"Nonsense!"

Flanking Sylvia, looking into the long mirror, Han and the saleswoman rejected the gray dress with quick shakes of their heads. But utterly beguiled by the elegance and sophistication of her figure in the glass, Sylvia assigned Han's lapse of taste to his recent melancholy. The bohemian look of the saleswoman, her sandals, bracelets and splashy tunic explained her objection.

"A flashy dress in court? Would you wear a flashy suit? No, you wouldn't!" Sylvia suspected again that Han was trying to sink her. His mood of intense preoccupation, his alarm at the endless interruptions of daily life could easily be the traits of a guilty person. But remembering that it was Han who'd persuaded Harry Rodman she should argue the motion and the way he'd worked with her, drilling her on the facts of the case, she decided that her suspicion was the outcome of her nerves. When tomorrow morning was finally over, her mind would clear and fill with trust.

"You know," Han smiled from the rack. "The model in the window is blond and short. Short, Sylvia."

"I can be short." She lifted her foot. "I'll substitute these horrible heels for an elegant pair of gray flats. New shoes will make this dress!"

Outside the dress store, Sylvia again looked through the window at the manikin in the simple gray dress. In its box, the weight of an identical dress pulled at her arm and she shivered with the thrill of magic. "I'll get those exact shoes!" This second purchase would complete her triumphant transformation into Han's noble wife.

"Those flats are stodgy, Sylvia! They don't express you at all." Han tugged her away from the window.

"Buy a pair of pumps with two-inch heels – no lower." He kissed her cheek and stepped away.

"Aren't you coming with me?" In her disappointment Sylvia barely understood that Han was going to the hospital for the second time that day to see his father.

"But he was irritated this morning by your visit. You said so."

"He just tires quickly, but he's really pleased to see me." Han turned away from Sylvia's sad skepticism.

"Will you be home tonight?"

"In an hour."

"An hour?" Sylvia looked at her watch. "Seven, then? You promise?"

"You bet!" Han called over his shoulder and hoped as he ran that Sylvia was admiring his speed and style.

The quick purchase of elegant gray pumps messed up Sylvia's spontaneous plan to visit two or three stores to buy the shoes and arrived home late, so that Han would already be there to greet her. But now he was visiting his father and the subway going home was sombre. Reflections on the loneliness of her life before Han moved in hit her hard, in waves.

Yet, after Han telephoned Alison the night before to say he was too sick to take the train home, Han came into the bedroom and announced that his marriage was over. From that night forward, he told her, all Alison wanted from him was enough money to support herself and their two sons. Sylvia worried that she should feel guilty about this development.

Han's news the next day, however, swept Alison out of Sylvia's mind, replacing concern with ambition. Since another case was taking Harry Rodman out of the country, they would be going before the judge without him in the first skirmish of their sex discrimination case.

"I should argue the motion."

Bounding up, taking her hand, Han had immediately agreed.

"Terrific! Excellent!" He pulled her past the naval prints that lined the narrow hall to Harry Rodman's office. The partner was on the telephone but waved them into the room. Han sat on the leather couch while she stood before the littered desk. Leaning back in his flexible chair, the partner's feet were up on the desk. As he ended his conversation, Han stepped up beside her.

"Harry, I think the case will be much better served if Sylvia argues the motion."

"What motion does she have in mind?" Harry Rodman reluctantly responded.

"Tell him, Sylvia."

"The motion about the dangerous documents." Sylvia's gaze rested on the partner's black shoes.

"Dangerous documents?"

"Dangerous resumés." Sylvia glanced back at Han, then smiled at Harry Rodman.

"Dangerous resumés?" The partner's eyes narrowed to slits, then opened in casual, almost lethargic interest. "I suppose there *is* a certain danger to one's sanity ... those files are so damn dull."

"I'm talking about the sexist comments written on the original resumé pages that you're trying to trick them out of seeing." Sylvia froze in the icy alarm of his gaze.

"What in god's name did they teach you at law school, young lady? I don't spend my time thinking of tricks and neither should you."

Taking her hand, Han swept her into the hall. "See you in a minute." Propelled past the naval prints by his push, Sylvia heard Han shouting until she closed the door of the conference room behind her.

"I'm going to be fired," she said when Han returned. A buoyant, graceful shape as he blocked the sun in the window, Han was a jazzy boy, then judicious as he sat down at the table and bent over a bunch of papers.

"The English have their parliament, the French their culture, and for us it's The American Corporation. The American Corporation is our contribution to civilization. Jesus! What an asshole!" Winking at her confusion, middle age peeled off his features and voice. "Every time I really look at Rodman these days, I want to rub that phony expression right off his face. What does he look like? That dark suit,' and that costly, muted tie. A funeral director? A pimp?" Han flung out an arm with a sly smile.

"A corporation lawyer. That's what Rodman looks like."

"That phony office. All that wood and leather. Christ, it's like a stage set – all so pretentious and self-important." Han swung down his legs and jumped up. "You're not going to be fired. You're arguing the motion!"

Later that night, however, Sylvia's hand trembled as she stood before her apartment door and turned the key. Her panic came on full again with the lock's loud click.

"I'm going to be fired," She informed the dark kitchen. "They're just setting me up." Rushing to turn on the Chinese lamp, she couldn't remember the responses that Han, at this point, would make to her litany. She could visualize Han's calm face, but his voice was drowned in her dread.

She'd stepped right into the trap! She was a joke to Harry Rodman and a damn nuisance as well. He planned to use her ambition to toss her away. Even if he didn't think she was stupid as mud, he knew her inexperience was dangerous. Why would he take such a chance? Because the motion wasn't important – Han was lying to her when he said it was – and, when she was crawling out of the courtroom, he'd be at the bench, setting things straight.

As Sylvia imagined Han's treachery, she unwrapped the gray dress and hung it reverently in the closet. The sight of the shoes set neatly beneath the hem finally brought the realism that Han's presence always imposed. She had the case down cold. She would shine in court.

Sylvia stepped up to the new dress and pushed back the bright clothes on either side. "There's some room, my lady." Grasping the soft material, she curtsied.

"I love you!" Had she really said that? Sylvia jerked around, but the room was empty.

CHAPTER 9

"I feel so spaced out!" Sylvia apologized as she again knocked into Han on the street. Wanting to see his face, she touched his arm, but he persisted in presenting his stern profile as they ducked into the subway. Twenty minutes beforehand, dressed for court, waiting for Han to come out of the bathroom, she'd imagined his kind face and the warmth of his tone so intensely, *that gray dress is terrific* – that his cold silence didn't fully register until she encountered it for a second time in the subway.

"Ridiculous shoes," he remarked, briskly, and jogged down the stairwell.

In the subway car she moved past Han to a space where she could see herself in the black window glass. Wasn't it weird to be feeling so different from the way she looked? She couldn't get enough of the elegant figure in the window. The dress looked as essential as skin and like a bird or cat, she appeared thoroughly organized, efficient and predictable. Why, then, was she feeling so diffuse?

Behind Han, ascending to the street again, the sensation grew stronger as she climbed and savored her sense of the surroundings. The gold cross of a church appeared in the square of sky at the top of the stairs, then its steeple, roof and columns, all as if launched on her strong breathing and headed for the wild blue yonder.

Compared to the marble halls of the Court House, the courtroom they entered was a cheerful, encouraging space. The Bench was a simple wooden desk set on a platform. The iron railing running a foot or so in front of it was the Bar. The place where the jury sat was a casual enclosure on the judge's left and there were two long tables on which the teams of opposing lawyers could spread out their papers. Between the tables, close to the judge and the jury box was a lectern from which the lawyers conducted their cases. As she followed Han, Sylvia heard a loud banging on the other courtroom door and saw an attendant go to the back of the room with a key. The handle rattled.

"What is this?" A voice fumed on the other side. A young woman nodded to the attendant as she stepped through the unlocked door and uttered a gruff "thanks." Going to the table opposite Han, she lifted up her briefcase and gave him a friendly smile. Her colorful silk dress, her carriage and stride expressed confidence, and Sylvia wasn't surprised to hear that the vivid, blond woman was Virginia Howe.

Watching her arrange her papers, Sylvia regained her faith in reality. The thick furniture and the lawyers' routine gestures assured her of her own physical validity. She was simple, solid and competent just like Virginia Howe. The sun shone strongly into the courtroom. Sylvia could see lint on the judge's robe when he entered and sat, and the edge of Virginia Howe's hair was a white flame as she walked to the lectern.

Virginia Howe spoke to the judge as though in friendly conversation. She was respectful and brief. She'd been ready to try this case for the past year. This was the third time that she'd argued against granting an extension to Moss and Poke and she honestly could not imagine their need for one. It was a small, straightforward affair and she hoped the Judge would allow the case to go ahead as scheduled, one week from today.

Han tapped Sylvia's shoulder as Virginia Howe sat down.

"Judge Feinberg is waiting to hear the motion," Han was gruff. "Let's go."

"Yes, let's!" Sylvia laughed at Han's stern face and pushed off from the table. Stilts, not legs, flung her at the lectern, and she held onto it for dear life. A friendly second chin appeared on the judge's face as he leaned on his hand and nodded at her to begin. His glasses sparkled with sunlight. His eyeglasses were sparkling with electromagnetic waves propelled through space at the speed of light. The light on his lenses was eight minutes old. Sylvia felt her brain had become a record of Han's jaunty lectures. Temporarily, the needle was as stuck, as were her eyes, on the phenomenon of light.

"Hey!" She cried, as Han stepped up beside her and started to speak.

When he kept talking, Sylvia let go of the lectern and leaned in front of him. "Hey, I'm supposed to do this."

"Can you?" He softly asked.

'Yes. Sit down!"

Her rage at Han burned up the script that was stored in her mind.

"I'm surprised I can talk," she smiled at the judge. "For the past twelve months I've felt like a miner, not a lawyer. Responding to the inquiries of Miss Howe, I feel I've crawled through miles of files. I've been trained to be thorough, your honor, and it takes time. Let me give you some specific examples of what we're up against …"

The moment Sylvia stopped speaking, her heart sent her blood so fiercely through her body that until the judge stepped through a door just behind the bench and the courtroom cleared, she was only aware of a general roar and glare. She looked cautiously at Han as he deftly packed the tote bag.

"You were terrific, Sylvia, much better than I would have been. You're the one to try the case and I'm going to tell Rodman so." He picked up the bag and started up the aisle.

"I panicked," she protested. "I wasn't professional."

"You were effective!'

"What do you mean?"

"The judge granted the extension."

"Why did the judge go our way?" Sylvia despaired as she hooked onto his arm. He hadn't yet looked at her. She'd insulted him in public and he was too proud to admit he was furious.

"I think I've caught your virus. I was a disaster."

In the cab to James Street, Han stroked her cheek and raved about her. She was a born litigator. The impression she gave of honesty and integrity was very rare and very useful and best of all she – was a money player.

"You know Rodman's favorite saying, 'all wars are won by sick soldiers'? Well, you didn't even know you were sick until the ordeal was over."

"I messed up and you know it."

"Messed up? You had the judge crawling through the files with you. That was wonderful! Original!" His frigid profile acknowledged her failure – why was he praising her? His diplomacy was making her nauseous. Sylvia took the gray dress into the bathroom. When she'd washed and brushed her teeth, she stepped out into the kitchen, the gray dress over her shoulder. Making tea, Han frowned.

"Get rid of it!" He growled.

Sylvia laughed as she felt the flow of his usual affection return.

"I can't stand that dress. You look great again."

Taking the tea, Sylvia felt the greatest relief of her life. Han's terrifying look was worry, not disinterest.

"Good tea."

"Good." He lifted the strap back on her shoulder, then sat and pushed it down again.

"Even if I hated you, I couldn't say no." She lay back. "But I love you! I adore you! More and more! The Greeks were so right to worship the body."

Sylvia stroked Han's face while he unbuttoned his shirt. She gripped and pressed the hard muscles that appeared as he swept off his clothes. She reached to feel his hot, velvety hardness.

Then, oh, damn it! Oh, why? Only a desolate tunnel of flesh slanted into her body, completely inert. The eager smell of his skin went into her nose while her ears filled with the words of his love. Yet the furious friction of a hundred years couldn't scrape the dullness from her walls. When Han froze with a pure, shrill cry, Sylvia thrust up against him and answered with a copied sound, but the word that escaped her was, "Mother!"

After a few moments silence, Han kissed her neck. "This has happened before – the invasion of your mother."

Sylvia smelled his hair, then covered his face with delicate kisses. "She keeps calling. I can't help it."

Regretfully, gently, Han pulled away from her. She could never have enough of his silent, generous affection. She drew up the sheet and watched him as he dressed. Tying his shoes, his eyes flashed up, then dropped.

"You always look at me doing all the little stuff," He smiled. "I have to stop myself from showing off."

"I'm going to tell my mother that I'm in love with you. She always asks, and up until now I've said no."

"Bad idea, I think."

"I agree." Sylvia raced ahead of Han's apprehension. "She'd be terrified we'd get married and these calls are tough enough as it is."

The weekly conversations ran on tracks. Sylvia knew every station along the way and since Han had moved in with her, she'd never escaped the full route.

First, pleasant inquiry. Was Sylvia still enjoying the company of her roommate? Incredulity next. The world her daughter inhabited, its values and standards might as well be described in a foreign tongue. Then envy. What a great relief to live cozily with a man as though with a woman, to have no responsibilities, no duties. How did Sylvia and her roommate cope with the sexual drive that existed in every man for every woman?

"We sleep with each other." She told her mother once in the sunny room, after Han had gone back to the office. She raised one bare leg off the bed and then the other in the long pause that followed the derailing after station number three.

"No, not like children, mother. You know."

As her mother shouted through three thousand miles of air, Sylvia stopped admiring her legs and swept the sheet up to her neck.

"We're friends, mother. He's helping me to be a good lawyer."

That young man was taking advantage of her! Why was she permitting this exploitation when she hated sex? Why now, when all during high school and college Sylvia had stayed away from boys, had preserved her mind and body for an elevated life? Sylvia was just like her. Like mother, like daughter. Sex made her mother vomit.

"You used to tell me this," Sylvia said. "A long time ago when I was little, didn't you tell me this?"

All her young life her mother had prepared her. The moment she'd laid her eyes on Sylvia's infant face her mother had seen the image of herself. She'd known of the marvelous brain before she'd heard a word from Sylvia's lips because it was her own brain recreated in her eldest daughter. From the beginning of Sylvia's conscious life, she'd heard the miserable story of her mother's wedding night, repeated like a bedtime story, her physical shame, the nausea that had vaulted her over her sleeping husband to vomit out the window of the hotel. Sylvia was like her! She was not an ordinary woman! She did not bow down to men! She hated sex!

Sylvia put down the receiver on her mother's last commandment.

"The invasion of your mother," Han had called it.

Holy hell, she didn't want her mother's wooden body, didn't want her rage. How dare that woman claim her before she'd claimed herself? The sunny room felt invaded.

But then, pity suddenly shook her. Her poor, embittered mother! Sylvia wouldn't boast of her escape, she wouldn't mention it – ever.

Sylvia grabbed a dress from the closet. Now that she knew her flesh to be the wood of her mother's bitter construction, she could build a proper house for the handsome soldier doll. Scrape away her captured flesh until she reached the nerve, and in the time that it would take, why, she'd continue to lie.

CHAPTER 10

The Doctor was frying eggs in the tiny kitchen of his restaurant, listening to Han's latest medical update from the hospital.

"My father's had every test in the book – all negative. There's no weight loss. In fact, last week he gained a pound." Han squinted at Doc. "Do you think my mother would be planning a trip to Phoenix tomorrow if there was any chance of cancer?"

"If the judge is clean, why do you feel so guilty?"

"I know it's insane. How could I hurt my father with a tennis ball? Christ!"

Han pressed his ears. "What is that hideous sound? The boiler? The furnace?" When Han and Sylvia first discovered his restaurant, Doc had drawn their attention to the sound of the subway cars that sped beneath them. But now, Han could only hear the rumble as a drone of accusation like the sound of X-ray machines.

"Your conscience?"

"I'm not guilty, Doc. How could I be? It's his irritation that's so exhausting. Mother's the one who's losing weight. She hasn't had a full night's sleep since he came home from the hospital. Thank god, she's getting away, but what nurse will put up with him? He'll go through one a night."

"Another drink?" Doc looked at Han, then at Sylvia, who covered her glass with her hand.

"So, your father wasn't always so irritable?"

Han admired the firm lines of Doc's face as he poured out the scotch.

"My father was wonderful! He's just not used to living with a pain in his back."

"Is it getting worse?"

Han shook his head. "He's feeling it more. Why shouldn't he? It's been four months since I hit him in the back with a tennis ball." Sylvia sighed. As if she hadn't been there and didn't have the story off by heart. Han could see her discomfort, but why didn't she realize that he wouldn't countenance her disbelief? His father did not have cancer!

Leaning against the bar, Doc looked at Han with kind puzzlement. "In my country, disease is a symptom of moral degeneration and we search our souls to discover the cause. As for age," he smiled. "We chew the leaves of a local curative herb known as "charm-flowers" and hardly grow old at all."

Han examined Doc's smooth, glowing face with passionate interest. "Are you in your twenties? Thirties?"

"On my next birthday, I shall be fifty-one."

"Didn't you think he was twenty-five?" Han gripped Sylvia's wrist. "Thirty, at the most. It's astonishing! Do you chew the charm leaves yourself?"

Every visible part of the restaurateur's body looked comely and strong. Han contrasted his father's withering form with a burst of hope.

"Well, for children, mothers mash up the petals and leaves with milk and poke them down their infants' throats. Adults press the leaves into juice."

"Charm leaves must slow the aging process," Han suggested to Sylvia. "Recently, for some reason, Dad has been aging extremely fast. But if he started eating charm leaves – but look at Doc," Han directed her incredulous gaze. "He looks half his age. I know my father won't become young again, but his back will heal. I'm not round the bend, Sylvia. You can't deny the doctor's amazing youth, can you?"

Han whipped his wallet from his jacket pocket. "Do you have some with you? Can I buy some?" Han glowed with excitement.

Looking from one to the other, Doc acknowledged Sylvia's suspicion with a wry smile.

"This young woman is very level-headed. She is thinking the way you would, Han, if you were not so upset about your father. You should say to yourself, this man is spinning out a fairy story to take my money. Isn't the mythical tree of life famous? Then, why haven't I heard of the charm flower? This man is taking advantage of my terror to sell me ordinary marijuana at a scandalous price."

"Oh, yes!" Doc poured Han another drink. "It's a homely weed with yellow leaves and an unpleasant smell. It grows high up in the mountains and people chew the leaves or make charm tea, or grind up the roots, if they can't take the smell, and eat it mixed up in other foods. They believe that it chases the jealous, malicious spirits out of their bodies. In this advanced country, physical degeneration has organic causes and the ingestion of charm would have no effect whatever."

"A placebo isn't keeping you young, Doc! You studied medicine at the Sorbonne. Oh, no!" Han rapped the bar. "There must be some chemical reason for its success."

"You know, Mr. Smith, it may be that for all my Western education I don't believe in the physical cause of disease. It's quite possible that, to me, cancer is the learned name for our insatiable greed."

"Sell me some, Doc. I don't care what it costs."

The Doc put his hands on his hips, drew in his breath and let out a deep, taut sound that Han felt in his stomach. "In my country, people make a pilgrimage to the mountains to gather the charm flower herb. They pick only enough to last a year, because the difficulty of the journey, the hardship of the climb, prepares the spirit for the charm's good effect. It is a transaction of faith, you understand, not money. I can't sell you any charm, but I shall be happy to give you what your father will need."

"Thanks," Han rolled his eyes sarcastically. "Your year's supply will suffice."

No less than on the evening when Doc paid for their dinner, Han resented Doc's generosity, then despised his own prejudice. Lightly poking the solid chest, Han looked around the small, empty bar. "I hope you do more business at lunch. Do you think you're going to make it?"

"If I can get another loan. These days the banks are so suspicious. "

"I'll loan you the money."

"I badly need five thousand dollars. Please keep that tempting wallet out of sight." Doc took his hand and held it.

"I'll write you a check."

"You haven't got that kind of money."

"A week ago, I couldn't have loaned you anything, but yesterday, the family banker informed me that I've got a fortune to invest as I please. It's a ploy to avoid the inheritance tax, but the money is mine and in another six months, I'll be a rich man."

Han explained to Doc that his sudden prosperity was a consequence of his father's hatred of Welfare Capitalism. His delight in depriving the loathsome social services of as much money as possible had led him to give half of it to his son before his death.

"If your Daddy doesn't want to give his money to the poor, then you'd better hang on to that five thousand."

"This place will bloom – I know it. You need a few more weeks to get known, maybe more. Really, this room is attractive, the food's great. I don't know why people still don't know where you are, but you couldn't be better located. I'd feel safe loaning you seven thousand."

"I'll take five."

Looking steadily into Doc's cheerful, challenging eyes, Han opened his wallet, pulled out a check, then reached in his pocket for a pen.

"I want it in cash."

Han pocketed his wallet and stood up. "Well, come to dinner tomorrow. Eight?" He wrote out the address. "Can Sylvia and I expect you? You'll be interested in the house. It was built by an abolitionist during the days of slavery. He built two houses, actually, and set them back to back. They're identical. We own them both but only live in one. Remind me to show you the tunnel that connects the two. We think it was part of the underground railroad that smuggled slaves from the South to Canada."

At every subway stop, in the brief periods when the noise of the travelling train didn't force Sylvia into a troubled silence, Han apologized for his glee and listened again to her attempts to annul it.

"This is James Street, Han. Damn it!" She groaned as he gaily kissed her goodbye. "Will you promise to tell your mother that tomorrow you're going to loan five thousand dollars to an eccentric Doctor to float his failing bar? What time will you be home? What time, Han? Do you hear me?"

"That was your stop!" He cried. "You've got to prepare for court tomorrow."

"You'll probably wander off the face of the earth tonight and I want you to hear my opening statement. I'll walk you to your house and then go back downtown."

"Don't think I don't understand what you're saying. You're right!" Han declared as they stepped out on the street. "But I know my father's going to heal like a baby. I'm so relieved!"

"What can I say? What can I do?" Sylvia cried. "You seem bewitched."

Han took her hand and through the pressure of his fingers tried to convey the certainty which Sylvia, understandably, couldn't pick up from his words. "Let's hear your opening statement."

Impressed by Sylvia's reasoning, Han led her along his parents' block. The street lamps were inadequately powered and cast only a faint light along the sidewalk. As they came up to his house, Sylvia dropped his hand and gestured for caution. Soon she was a pace or two behind him, almost hidden in the dark.

"Want to go out tonight?" A woman was at Sylvia's elbow, walking with her as she looked at Han. Her coat was long, and she wore a wide brimmed hat. She darted to Han.

"Hey darlin', want to go out tonight?" I want to go out with you! Is that your girlfriend?" She trilled as Han looked back at Sylvia. "Oh, sorry! That's your girlfriend. Sorry sweetie," she dropped back to Sylvia. "I didn't know he was with you."

Smiling, Sylvia looked back as the woman retreated down the street into shadow. "That's okay."

Frowning at Sylvia's inappropriate warmth, Han opened the gate.

"That was so strange, Han!" Oddly mournful, Sylvia kept looking over her shoulder. "She must have known we were together. Why do you think she's working this neighborhood?"

"A bit crazed? Maybe drugged?" Han waved down a cab. "Poor woman."

"But Han, those respectable clothes. Why this upscale, deserted neighborhood?" Sylvia settled into the cab. "Don't forget to tell your mother all about the miraculous charm flower. Promise?"

Sylvia blew him a kiss as the cab sped off. The handle of the front door of his parent's town house felt heavier than usual and Han found himself admiring, as he hadn't since childhood, the dignity of the carved door. On the vacations which brought Han home from boarding school and college it had been his custom to greet the house and yard before calling out to his parents. The sound of his mother's plaintive voice, speaking into the telephone in her upstairs sitting room, was usually present, just as it was now, while Han happily absorbed the welcome of the empty rooms. The dining room table set with the household's best china for his homecoming dinner would seem to him the essence of gracious affection.

Tonight, the table was bare, but he could see beyond to the

pantry counter that held his father's dinner. He opened the garden door and stepped out onto the terrace.

Enclosed by the back of the twin house opposite and the two brick side walls of the neighboring houses was a yard, which even Han, in the grip of nostalgia, could see was too narrow for the swimming pool he'd once begged his father to install. A cube of chilly water in the middle of a sweltering city had seemed as exciting to Han as an oasis in a desert and his father's compromise of a wading pool had made him briefly ill with disappointment.

But the installation of the pool had led to a grimly thrilling discovery. The first hour of digging had exposed the roof of an underground tunnel running from one house to the other just a foot beneath the grass. The yard's eventual landscaping included flowering bushes and in the warm months of the year, the water in the pool reflected the backyards of both houses, their images merging in a constant confusion of likeness.

Tonight, the empty pool looked as large as it had in his childhood. So did the yard. The twin houses seemed even taller and the square of light from his father's bedroom window was again the beacon of his youthful devotion.

As Han walked back through the yard and house and climbed the stairs to the upstairs hall, his knees felt chilly as though he was again wearing the shorts of his early childhood. A reading lamp was clamped to the headboard of his father's bed. Its light fell on a messy pile of newspapers and books. The judge no longer read in bed, but angrily sighed as his legs constantly moved beneath the bedclothes.

"Good god!" Judge Smith pointed to the yellow tie that Sylvia had bought Han. "I know the firm's taking people whose names I can't even pronounced these days, but they can't be wearing ties like that! "

"I like it." Helplessly, Han stretched his fingers over the tie.

"How are you feeling?"

"It is idiotic of you to ask me that every time you see me.

Until I tell you different, you may assume that I feel like hell. Your mother's in her room."

Han tried to obey the command that he greet his mother, but his father's shrill rage hooked him back.

"Bradford Poke came to see me the other night. He wanted to sing your praises but was terribly embarrassed because he couldn't remember what case you're working on. He was astonished when I told him and wondered if I had it right. He was well aware of a young woman associate who's so good she's breaking all the rules, but your obscurity made him feel like a idiot. Why aren't *you* burning up the track?"

"You're talking about Sylvia Stride, dad. We're a team. I prepare the case and she argues it." His father's silent contempt reminded Han how hard he'd always run. Unlike Sylvia, who wanted to race, he was in flight. "She's a strategy, dad. Remember that the case is a sex discrimination suit. It was my idea to have a woman try it."

The shame of betraying Sylvia was strong but bearable. But the fear of losing his father's respect was intolerable. He was surprised at the clarity of this recognition, like a flair of lightening in a murky sky.

"That makes sense if she's any good at all."

"I see to it that she is."

"Why aren't you downtown? When I was your age, I worked every night. "

His father's pride renewed Han's ambition. The following day, Harry Rodman was going to hear Sylvia in court for the first time. To be sure she'd shine, to really knock him out, they needed a few more hours of work. Han looked at the clock on the dresser and took a step towards the door.

"I was younger than you when I got my first assignment from Alex Moss. I worked straight through the weekend and on Monday morning I surprised the hell out of him by having the memo on his desk when he came in. Three hours later, he wanted to see me. Always puffing on his cheap cigars, he was reading the memo when I came through his door. 'I didn't think you could do this,' he said to me. 'Not a bad job.'" The judge glared at Han. "You left the office yesterday afternoon. You're here now."

"I'm on my way downtown." This latest reminder of his father's intellectual endurance, his stamina for pain, revved Han up to an urgency of imitation. He edged towards the door.

"If you've been so stupid as to come – stay!"

"Sylvia and I have a lot of ground to cover before the morning."

"Sylvia? Your secretary?"

"Sylvia's the brilliant young associate. You know! She was my tennis partner the evening Alison was in Europe."

"I'll give you a rematch if you're up to the challenge. Alison played very well that night. I'm sorry not to see more of her. She's one of the most attractive young matrons I know. It's a damn tricky business – " He breathed with a sharp gasp and stared at the ceiling. Drying his face with the edge of the sheet he sat up, forlorn and embarrassed.

"By the way – I hope you know what you're doing about that tree upstate. It's too close to the house to cut it down. You know how your mother feels about trees – she's in a state." He lifted himself with both hands, his forehead wet with sweat. "Dr. Adams told me to exercise my back. Your mother wants me to go to Phoenix with her. Tells me it's simple to get another ticket." Panting, he wiped his face. "The fox wakes up on the hour and when he's chewing my insides I'd rather be in my own bed."

"I've found this doctor, Dad. He's sure he can help you. I'm bringing him to see you tomorrow night."

"Doctors," he softly fumed. "Bring a murderer, why don't you. There! The fox has stopped. If you're going – go!"

Han stepped from foot to foot. "I think I should."
The next day Han carried Doc's money in a taxi from the bank to the brownstone house and hid it in his old room. Downtown at his

desk, thoughts of the platter of lamb and potatoes that the cook had promised, the red tulips in the window of the corner flower shop and the cheese and éclairs that he intended to buy for Doc's dinner made everything within the walls of Moss and Poke seem a flimsy stage set. It was conceivable, as the sun went down, that this special evening would be a launch to infinity. Released from the stream of continuity, Han would never be back.

At eight o'clock, Han opened the front door and stood waiting on the steps. The streetlights were so dim that Doc needed guidance into the house, then up the dim stairs and into his father's bedroom. Although his father had agreed to hear out this man, his wrathful face on seeing Doc terrified Han and he fled down the stairs and out the front door.

Han ran up and down the block until he was too tired to be afraid and finally sank down in his parents' small courtyard.

The cook was preparing his father's supper tray. Every evening the illusion of robust health was created by the quantity and variety of the dishes served. Han's mother was grave and meticulous as she lifted covers, sniffed and took tiny bits of food on a finger as though to guard against the poisoning of her mate. The lamb was in the warming oven, double boilers packed the stove and his father, with his furious feet, was groaning in his bed.

"My son is a damn fool, sir. When he was a youngster, I made him drop his shorts once a week. Beating sense into him was a Saturday chore of mine. But I never succeeded. One week he'd dig a crater in the back yard looking for treasure, the next, a bush would be destroyed because of a pair of mail order wings that he thought would enable him to fly. I remember the 'invisible' ink in the upstairs hall that cost a fortune to paper over. There's a great deal more that comes to mind, but you, Sir, are apparently the most current example of Han's absurd gullibility."

Having labeled Doc a member of the great class of quacks, Judge Smith sank down in bed, too tired to refine his initial classification.

"I can imagine your anger at being stopped by a cynical old man. I give you fair warning." Pushing forward, the judge pointed his finger at Doc. "If you've lied your way in here in order to set this house up for a robbery, I'll have you behind bars for the rest of life."

'Your honor." Doc's huge hands swept up and came together on his chest. His chin rested on his fingertips as smiling he looked down with mischievous, almond-shaped eyes. "What else can I be but what you believe?"

Panting as he strained, Judge Smith again sat upright. "You don't fool me, sir. Flowing robe, English accent, man's earring, speaking like a goddamned oracle. You're either involved in narcotics or revolution, most likely both. And yet, here you are, let into the house by my son because he's a god-damned credulous idiot!"

Han was just turning up the heat under the double boiler and checking the lamb. Seeing Doc, he reached into the cupboard for glasses. Doc's hand settled on his shoulder.

"How did it go?" He smiled, surprised by the man's evident sympathy. Doc pointed at the ceiling.

"Mean, Han. Very mean."

"Not personal, though." Han put a drink in Doc's hand. "Dad liked you, if anything, It's the damn pain."

"Me? What do I care? It's you."

"Me?" Han laughed with relief. "I enjoy Dad. I hope you did."

"You looked rocky," Doc clicked Han's glass with his own. "I couldn't help but notice."

"Well, his frankness, I was worried how you'd take it."

"When he said you were a damn fool. Your face – I wanted to kill him!" Doc's eyes were luminous and loathing. "He's malignant, Han! The sickest soul I've ever seen!"

"You're seeing the pain! Really! Dad was wonderful before he hurt his back. Come on!" Han beckoned and pushed against the kitchen door. "I'll show you some pictures."

Han closed the library door and sat Doc behind his father's huge mahogany desk. Swiftly considering as he went around the book-lined room, he lifted three framed photographs off the wall, then placed them one by one in Doc's hands.

As Doc silently handed the first two back to him, Han was glad that the best proof of his father's splendor had been saved for last. Bending at Doc's shoulder, the sight of the young army captain with unflinching, regal eyes affected Han profoundly. Proudly taking Doc's silence for respect, Han hung the three photographs back up on the wall. "Dad was the youngest captain in the Army. He tells great stories."

The silver letter opener, the ivory cigarette box, the jade elephant from India appeared and disappeared in Doc's big fists. Frowning and sighing, his attention wandered over the desk top and the bookcases that lined the room. He got up to look at the silver tennis cups and the tiny statues made of precious stones that Judge Smith had collected in his travels around the world.

"I'm retrieving this, if you don't mind." Han plucked the jade elephant from Doc's palm and put it back on the desk. "Five thousand bucks is enough for one night, for god's sweet sake. Come on! You're going to love this lamb."

Doc drank and ate with jovial persistence until Han was digging at the bone for rosy bits of meat. As many times as he carved at the sideboard and filled Doc's plate with food, he helped them both to his father's best wine. Doc's casual dignity and his enormous appetite inspired Han to an ecstasy of hospitality. He loved putting food on his plate.

"Treasure?" Doc turned from the table and crossed his legs. "How'd you happen to be hunting for treasure?"

Han told the story of that long ago spring afternoon when his father – to get rid of him, it was now obvious – told him the legend of a runaway cabin boy from one of his great-grandfather's ships, who buried a purse full of gold coins somewhere in the small yard.

He described how it was reasoned out between them what the most likely spot would be, and how Han, in a frenzy of excitement, had dug until his hands were too blistered to grip the shovel – only to finally face his father's eruption of sarcastic pleasure.

"Can you believe I was that stupid?" His elbow on the table, he held his head and looked fearlessly into Doc's face. "Dad couldn't. But he didn't beat me. He just laughed and told mother. They had a cocktail party that night and I heard him telling everyone about my futile quest for buried treasure."

"You were how small?" Doc put out his hand, palm down, and nodded at Han with absorbed eyes. When Han said he'd been eight years old at the time, Doc pondered the small space between his hand and the floor.

Han put a humidor filled with cigars between them on the table and Doc touched the ivory inlay, looked dreamily at the sideboard crowded with silver dishes and finally fixed his eyes on the great candlestick in the center of the table.

"I need your bathroom."

In the hall, coming back, Doc's voice rang with the indifferent certainty of a chant. "Silks, satins, ivory and jade."

He took up his cigar as he sat and filled his mouth with smoke. "Precious silks and satins, ivory, jade," his hand opened to reveal the tiny elephant from India, "gold and silver – this house is bursting with treasure. Hundreds of years of colonizing to get at the metals and then transform them to such beautiful things. If it were just the things," he put the elephant on the table beneath one of the candlestick's silver arms, "if it were only for the making of such exquisite stuff that all the greed and bullying occurred it might be tolerable. If the idea of paradise was looking at a majestic silver candlestick, or an enamel box inlaid with gold, if the greed were finally transformed to joy, then perhaps there'd be no fuel for revolution."

The flash of his father's face and voice in Doc's quick monologue left Han smiling in discomfort.

"But when the man in the bed upstairs looks around at his loot, he sees only symbols of his success and he's furious because another judge has six majestic candlesticks and he has only one. In another man's house, the loot in all its lovely transformations fills him with anger and envy. He sees only ornaments to another man's grandeur, and he rages like a jealous god."

"I never thought of it that way". Han followed Doc's amused eyes to the graceful candlestick.

"Neither did I." Doc's shoulders shook as he silently laughed. He poked the jade elephant until its trunk touched the base of the candlestick. "To children, certain things are magical. That fellow there," he tapped the elephant's head, "he reminds me of how I used to feel, because the same year I carved an elephant for my mother, I wanted a new bicycle for myself. It would tire me in a minute to want something so badly now, but were I to find that bike beside my bed one morning, I know I'd still feel the joy."

Every time Doc looked up, the silver candlestick roused a passionate admiration.

"I hope you'll accept the elephant. My father will never miss it."

"Thank you." Doc picked up the tiny beast and put it down. "I'd rather steal it."

Han glanced at the ceiling. "To the judge, you already have."

Doc's silent amusement, his thick, shaking shoulders so delighted Han that he opened another bottle of the marvelous wine. Having aimed all night for the clarity and distance that set in at a certain stage of drinking, Han suddenly put down his glass, tossed back his head and finally dared to ask Doc how he found his father.

"If you hadn't shown me those photos, I'd have given my wares a better chance. Sick from meanness, mean from sickness, perhaps it doesn't matter. Now, show me that tunnel you were telling me about."

Han stared at the small, yellow envelope that Doc drew from his tunic and put down on the table. He touched it with his finger.

"How do you use it?"

Doc's voice sent strong shivers through Han's body as he explained that to achieve the maximum effect the charm should enter the body through a vein.

"Does one always use needles?"

"It has not been the custom until recently and now only with the young men. Smiling, the doctor swept to his feet. "Please, the tunnel."

At the top of the cellar stairs, a narrow, white-painted space sprang at them as Han switched on the light. Doc stepped in front of him and went slowly down the stairs, his head turning as he looked. "Orderly, admirable, well done," he touched the tools that were hung on the wall. He picked a flashlight off a shelf and laughed with satisfaction at the flow of a strong beam. Doc swept the light over the bricks of a low archway.

The furnace clicked on, entrancing Han with its solid, mellow hum. As Doc bent before a moldy wooden door, feeling with his fingers and sniffing at the crack, Han pressed his head against the side of the humming furnace and was delighted by the triumphant music that in drunkenness he was able to hear. Moving his ear along the metal, Han discovered violins and trumpets, their sound intensely oscillating in the steel.

The low, ancient door had no handle. Mold had softened the wood, which exploded in a burst of green as Doc's fist burst the door open. Bending over, his body completely filled the narrow tunnel and blocked the beam that shone from the flashlight in his hands.

His hands on his knees, Han stooped and peered. Doc's broad, toiling backside, his excited grunts repelled him. Wiping away the greasy, cold air of the tunnel which covered his face like decay, Han sprang for the stairs. The violins soared as he passed the furnace. Hauling himself up along the banister, taking the stairs in bunches, the yellow envelope left on the dining room table was a brilliant light in his mind.

CHAPTER 11

"She did a nice job today – exactly what was needed – and she's still calling me Sir."

"Maybe Sylvia thinks you're the shoeshine boy."

Slowly Harry Rodman's tough eyes settled on Han. "I don't get it."

Han had been tapping his foot and drumming on the table since supper began. Now he flipped his spoon in the air and caught it with a grin.

"You once told me that Virginia Howe chewed gum, put her feet up on the desk and called no man 'Sir' but the shoeshine boy." Han looked at the partner with affection. "You felt you'd been obtuse not to realize at that point she was a troublemaker."

In the crowded restaurant, the wave of male laughter was continual.

Han's mirth pierced the mild roar like the shriek of a sea bird. Sitting across from Han, Sylvia avoided his mocking eyes.

"Virginia Howe refused to work in Trusts and Estates. She's a very dangerous character. "Those pants, today! Those boots! God damn Cossack."

"She looked terrific!" Han challenged. "She's a beautiful woman."

Small red spots animated Harry Rodman's face and his breathing grew wet. "What chivalry," he at last intoned, "that woman has no case. The jury's going to throw her personal grudge right out of court."

"Come on, Harry. When Sylvia was buried in the files last

summer, she fished out our monkey tricks." Grinning, wagging his finger, Han ignored her silent plea to shut up.

"What did you tell me last summer? You correctly said that our defiance was blatant obfuscation."

"I did?" She measured the partner's livid distrust out of the corner of her eye. "I didn't know I could pronounce it."

"Sylvia didn't know she could pronounce it." Han addressed the partner with soft disgust. "But she can do it, Harry, brilliantly. By the way, there's something I should tell you."

Sylvia gripped the edge of the table as her worst fear transpired. With a light air of authority derived from god knows where, Han was telling Harry Rodman that he planned to take next week off and look after his father.

"But this trial is terribly important!" Harry Rodman protested, breathing hard.

"There's nothing tricky in the next few days as you know. But, anyway, our friend here is on top of it. She's an ace!" Han's bold tone, as he picked up the check and strode toward the cashier, stunned the partner.

"Is his father dying? The old guy must be dying."

Han spun round with a smile. "He's feeling better, Harry. Much, much better!"

"Where were you at the Battle of Armageddon, Smith? Making milk toast and playing checkers in a convalescent home? If your father wants a nurse, he sure as hell doesn't want you! "

Getting out his wallet, waiting for his change, Han's bright, teasing smile kept fading in the face of the partner's rage, then broke out anew. Sylvia thought she would drown in the waves of Harry Rodman's fury, but Han was a surfer, smiling and fleet.

"You'll compromise your chances at the firm, Han."

Back in their office, Sylvia checked the empty hall and leaned on the door after the soft click of the lock. "Didn't you see how he looked? You can't just up and take a week off."

His foot up on the radiator, leaning on his knee, Han was looking out the window. All she saw of his face was a forbidding profile. Reaching, he rapped the wall, his desk, then the glass. He rubbed his knuckles as he stared at the view. "Plaster, glass, wood, just as always. It all just looks as if it's painted on. The problem with me is getting worse all the time. But Harry Rodman, dangerous? He's an old sea bass. It's all underwater, all so slow and murky — very important if you happen to be a fish." Han sighed and pulled his ear. "Virginia Howe is believable, because she's drowning, poor woman."

That afternoon, presenting the case, Sylvia had continually looked at Han for support but his eyes were anywhere but on her. Quite often, they were on Virginia Howe and with a plunge of her heart, Sylvia would feel she was speaking like an actress who didn't understand her lines. This afternoon, Sylvia could hardly wait to get Han's reaction to her opponent's grimly murmured outburst. Surely, it would interest Han to hear themselves characterized in open court as a bunch of white-collar crooks. But on the courthouse steps, Han could only groan that the square of judicial buildings with fringes of Greek columns was unbearably pompous.

"You are jealous," she stormed, then stopped, for his incomprehension appeared sincere. But wasn't it obvious that her former cynicism and his current loss of faith were not objective perceptions of the case, but simply the reflections of their reversed positions? How else could she explain the flip of her attitude about the same set of facts? What had changed except that now she, not Han, was Harry Rodman's favorite? And at weekends now, Han was so different.

All week she yearned for Saturday and the return of his affectionate gaze. Swiping one of his shirts and a pair of jeans, she'd shower and push open the bathroom door to his invariable cheer. She looked great, he'd tell her. Looked herself for the first time all week. God, he hated her new sober clothes.

Oh, yes. Weekends really were the proof of his jealousy, because once away from the office, she was never perplexed by his restlessness and she never had to rouse him from the daydreams that endangered their work. If she could only board up that office window, she'd tell him, they might get a regular evening at home for a change. Surprised at his lapse, always apologetic, he'd tear his eyes from the harbor and go back to preparing her for the next day on her feet. Tensing when he praised her performance, Sylvia heard only, "goodbye, goodbye,"

"You said Virginia Howe was a beautiful woman."

"Harry Rodman told me that when she worked here, she wore pants – not pants suits, but bright slacks and shirts – gypsy clothes, he called them. She used to put her feet up on her desk and she chewed gum – just like you did before you turned respectable."

"How dare you tell Harry Rodman that I said our defense was "obfuscation"?" Sylvia raced into rage. "You hate it that's it me who's trying the case and you're going to sink me. You will sink me, you damned hypocrite!"

Han's hands clasped his head. "Why do you hate yourself so much?"

"I was brought up to. My mother was proud. She said that self-hatred is the fuel of ambition and the way to achieve self-control."

"It is pride, isn't it? The proud masochist. You should stop it."

"So I can be like you?" She shouted. "You run out on your wife and you don't even call."

"I tried to call. The phone is disconnected."

"She's probably in the hospital."

"Our doctor hasn't heard from Alison. I've called him several times."

"She's broke then. She can't pay her telephone bills."

"I always deposit my paycheck in her account. She's certainly not in want of money."

"I wonder how much I'll get when you start your affair with Virginia Howe?"

"Wall Street is driving you crazy, Sylvia. You're losing it."

"Hypocrite!"

Han laughed and stretched. "Once upon a time there was a young woman who wanted to be a litigator. When she was hired by Moss and Poke and put to work on a case, she was so thrilled that months passed before she realized that she wasn't."

"Shut up, shut up, shut up," she softly chanted, as Han, calmly accurate, recited back the drastic self-prophecy that she'd thought she'd spoken only to the air.

"Passed over for a partnership," he raised his forefinger and his voice as Sylvia ran to the door and opened it. "That she could have been so stupid, so blinded by ambition – "

Relieved by the empty hall, Sylvia kicked shut the door, picked up a small book and scaled it into Han's chest.

"I'm not that person anymore! I'm not a loser, a Virginia Howe – anymore!"

Han rubbed his chest. "Do you like that asshole calling you 'she' when you're sitting at the same table with him?"

"It's not personal."

"It's okay by you that he thinks you're his puppet? That he only trusts you because he assumes you're stupid? You go along with that?"

"I'll never get to be a partner if Harry Rodman doesn't think I'm dumb. Stop laughing. I'll kill you if you don't stop laughing, because you shouldn't laugh at me, because you know my only chance is playing it this way – until he really trusts me. Shut up!" She burst into tears. "It's outrageous the difference between us because of external things. It's un-American and you're a rat to laugh."

"Outrageous, indeed." Han was sadly sympathetic. "But you can't fight it here. Don't you see, Sylvia? Stupid associate, stupid young partner, stupid head of the firm. You've got to get out."

"But where?" She looked frantically around the room. "It's the same everywhere."

"Look at Virginia Howe. She's putting up a hell of a fight."

"Because she didn't make it!" Hatred flooded her. "She's a loser even if she wins! This is what counts. People know about *this*."

"I'll help you."

"You're taking the week off," she shouted. "You' re a loser like her. That's why you love her."

"You love her too, but I'll help you." His hand shot out to grab the ringing telephone. Staring at her, the receiver pressed against his shoulder, he insisted "You're the darling of my soul. Trust me."

Sylvia's trust was swift and physical. Her blood tingled in her spine and stomach. Han loved her – not Virginia Howe.

The office window grew black behind him as Han, in the exultant tone of the past few days, announced to his mother in Phoenix that he was about to clean and repaint the fishpond. "I'll be taking my vacation until you get home. You won't recognize the backyard or Dad."

"The charm flower," Sylvia whispered as Han hung up the phone. She clung to her happiness as she stood. "Did Doc take your money?"

"It's effective, Sylvia. There's been a wonderful change. Dad's eating more, sleeping better and even reading. He's down two pounds from last week, the doctor says, but he expected that."

"Don't worry about the case. We'll still work at night. You'll love my old room on the third floor. I've cleaned it like crazy and pushed the beds together. You'll love staying in an old brownstone. Don't fret!" Han cried in a rapture. "It's a wonderful house!"

"There's going to be some surprise at the hospital when they run those tests on Dad." Han served Sylvia more stew. "On Monday," he reveled, passing back her plate.

Bolts of cold closed up Sylvia's stomach, for on Monday, the judge would be staring down on a fright-frozen idiot. An idiot's nod as Harry Rodman whispered in her ear, an idiot's stare while the courtroom filled with the silence of alarm.

"Sylvia, eat!" Han pointed at her plate. "You need your strength."

Catalyzed by Han's voice, the voice of his wife became dominant in Sylvia's mind. In the narrow dining room, lit only by the five candles set in the silver candelabra that so persistently held Doc's eyes, Sylvia felt a minute of exquisite warmth, as though the summer sun was racing down through miles of pure air. Wasn't Sylvia the equal of any man? But she must eat! Coughing as the vision passed, Sylvia longed to get into her own bed where every night Alison's imagined praise and touch soothed her to a hero's sleep.

"Sylvia's been coughing like that since yesterday afternoon," Han said to Doc. "I wish you'd take a look at her throat."

Intending to shield Doc from a distasteful task, Sylvia rejected the idea. She supposed she must be coughing from nerves – there certainly was no physical cause.

"On Monday, when I don't know what to say, I'll just cough." She squinted at Han. "I'll obfuscate."

Sipping coffee during the weekend, taking notes from the trial transcript and quizzing Han while he painted the fish pool, she continued to be firmly enclosed in the capsule of Monday's dread. Surprised, then impatient, the judge would stare down at a sweating statue. But to observe Han's derangement in her nightmarish state was a benefit too. His father's sudden agony, Han's frantic telephone call to Doc and his writing out of a thousand-dollar check, his happy display to her of a fragile, gray faced man, who in a hollow voice called out "Alison" – through it all Sylvia marveled at the numbing anesthesia provided by her approaching doom.

The sky was a deep blue while Han applied the coats of weatherproof paint. As white as the paint, clouds like castles slipped west. On Sunday evening, fixing the plastic drop cloth as Han directed, the tops and sides of the clouds glowed in the sunlight the city had turned beyond. At home beyond the mountains it was still early afternoon - but Sylvia knew she mustn't think about home because she couldn't get in the door again without a medal.

CHAPTER 12

Fear pulled so strongly through Sylvia's body that when Virginia Howe left the lectern and the judge looked in her direction, the normal pressure of her feet on the floor was only good for a few seconds before she dropped back in her chair. Pushing with her hands, standing and walking, her mind flashed a picture of Han and Virginia working together in a small, sunny office. Then a gay, congratulatory wind played round her as she crossed the floor.

"It was okay – not bad at all," Sylvia later telephoned to Han. "It was thin ice all morning. Harry Rodman looked ill – but we made it." She laughed at Han's enthusiasm, but her hands shook hard. She'd intended to relate the moment of her reprieve, the moment that she dared look past her doom and saw that the judge was not listening to a lunatic, that his face, in fact, looked sharp with comprehension, but instead she reported: "Virginia Howe's got nice legs. The slit in her skirt went almost to her underpants – so she could swim, I suppose. You said she was drowning," she teased his bewilderment. "Don't you remember?"

It completed her happiness that he did not, and she never thought to ask why he wanted her to pick up a phonograph needle on her way to the judge's house.

At the fourth music store the correct diamond needle was finally in her purse and elation swept her uptown. Letting herself into the house, Sylvia walked into a spicy smell of Doc's cooking. The dining room table was set for three and she couldn't help her hostility.

Grabbing her hand, Han pulled her into the kitchen. "Didn't I say you'd be terrific?" He poured water from the kettle into the bottom of the double boiler and opened the oven door.

"Another twenty minutes and you'll be eating the best sea bass you ever tasted." In a crouch before the stove, Han continued talking over his shoulder. "Doc brought his speakers. Dad's lost another three pounds, so I've got to turn his mood around. He's always loved music!"

"Have you given up on that charm stuff?"

"God, no! Dad's such a tough case, Doc's rounding up some more."

"For another thousand?"

"It's effective. Do you have the needle?"

Sylvia's morning freeze came back at the alarm in his eyes. Placing the crisp plastic box in his hand she hurried after him.

Judge Smith lay sleeping on a stack of pillows. He woke into exhaustion as Sylvia stepped up to the bottom of the bed.

"Alison, dear," he beckoned her to his side. "The tree fell right, did it? There will be plenty of sun now and enough firewood for a decade. Sad. Very sad."

All that remained of the athletic man who had cheated her in tennis was the thickness of his now white hair. The rest of him — skin, voice, muscle and bone — evinced an ancient being.

"Better," he gasped, when Han had shot the charm into his vein. "Much, much better." He caught Han's wrist and looked gratefully up into his face. "What was all that fooling around under my bed?" He smiled when Han explained. "No, I don't want Bach now. While you're downstairs devouring that delicious fish I shall listen to the evening news — as always." When Han looked back from the door, the judge gave him a relaxed wave.

Although outwardly calm as he brought in the fish and vegetables and poured the wine, Sylvia could feel Han's excitement. Her suspicion that Doc was the cause killed her appetite and the delicate, steaming fish went untasted to her stomach. She jealousy bowed her head until the silence encouraged a sneaky glance. Han was looking between Doc and herself. Absently, barely acknowledging her thought, Sylvia wondered what had happened to the huge silver candlestick.

"With those speakers of yours, Doc, the vibrations ought to sink right through my father's back. It was great of you to bring the needle." Han's excited face leaned to Sylvia. The judge's approval was shining on Han like a strong light.

"I've been reading dad a book on physics and I got this idea – obvious, really, I think – dentists make use of the structural similarity of sound and pain."

That night, after dinner, Han was going to try an experiment that was based on the theory that pain had a vibrational pattern which moved along the route of the nervous system in waves. He reached for her wine glass to demonstrate. "Too small."

Charging up, he took a silver bowl from the sideboard, filled it with wine and set it down next to her plate. The warmth of his side distracted her as he leaned, and she didn't understand why he was wiggling his forefingers in the bowl of wine.

"Say that again?" She murmured when he wiped off his fingers with a hopeful look.

"Do you see how each finger makes a wave? Now, watch the two waves approach and penetrate each other. Do you see how the wave motion is quenched whenever the crest of one wave falls into the trough of another?"

"It gets flat."

Han smiled at her genius. "Couldn't that same quenching of motion be established by sending, for example, a system of vibrations from the speakers under the bed to the surface of dad's back where they would penetrate and meet the emerging pain waves, crests tumbling into troughs, all motion, therefore all pain, erased?"

"Can sound waves penetrate?"

Han's eyes clung to the doctor's dark glasses and he repeated what Doc said. "If there's enough volume."

"If there's enough volume?" Sylvia came ruefully into the round. "If it's loud enough, I suppose you do feel sound. It's a force."

Han joyfully nodded. "I've had four speakers in action around his bedside and tonight I expanded the system by putting Doc's two under Dad's bed. God, what a sound it will be. First, Bach, I think. Those shattering boy sopranos and E. Power Biggs at the top of the scale. I'll penetrate his spine with the most idealistic aspect of the culture that Dad loves and annihilate those pain waves – mash them flat!"

"Don't you think, Han, don't you think that with all that's known about cancer these days, that if sound waves were helpful, they'd be a common therapy?" She stopped when she saw Han's reaction. "What's the matter?"

"Dad's got a back problem, Sylvia. If it was cancer I would have told you so."

"He's losing weight now, Naturally, I thought –"

"With my father, all it indicates is that he's not eating enough. Yesterday, all he got down was a poached egg and half a chicken breast. Doc suggests increasing his dose of charm with two extra shots before lunch and dinner. In between meals I'll be experimenting with various vibrational patterns until I come up with a winner. Do I hear him?" Han went to the door. "Hang on, you two, I'll be right back."

"It's obvious Judge Smith is dying," Sylvia turned to Doc, "Han's so gullible."

"Do you disapprove of his gullibility?" Doc addressed her with a pleasant smile.

"All the money you're taking from him. The way he deserted the case, I could easily dismiss him as a fool."

"And he'd still love you, wouldn't he? Just the way he loves that cruel man, his father."

"I'm not like his father!" Sylvia gasped with surprise and pain. "I'm not!"

"You don't confuse what you want with the way things are. You don't mix love and reality. You drive hard and in any job you will always advance." Amiably, Doc indicated his total disinterest in her existence. "I adore Han for his faith."

"It's so disgraceful, this indulgence, on both your parts. Faith, is it? You swindler."

They both jumped at the thunderous sound of an organ above their heads. Doc gazed at the ceiling and pressed his wine glass against his smiling mouth. "The windows will crack, the walls tumble, all pain shall die."

"Cocaine, heroin, whatever you're cheating him with, when you've picked him clean and he's ruined his career, you'd better give Han a job."

"Have faith!" Doc laughed.

Yanking up the plates and noisily stacking them, Sylvia hurried from his greasy prophet's voice and his glowing, upturned face.

The window over the sink went up easily and Sylvia leaned for a bit when the dishes were washed, her face pushed out into the warm, moist air. Buried in shrubbery by the corners of the house, spotlights subtly lit the elegant garden. The shadow boughs lunging along the back wall of the opposite house imparted a sense of momentum to the steamy kitchen. Swiftly the house bore down on its twin.

Later, when the kitchen was clean as a hospital laboratory and Doc had returned to his downtown bar, upstairs Han was reading to his father. Sylvia sat on the stairs outside the Judge's bedroom, deliberately drinking up a lust and admiring Han's intelligent voice.

"Is it possible that all of the different particles might be different states of motion of some underlying structure or substance?"

"Some underlying structure or – state?" Sylvia murmured to

herself. If Han this very moment should sink into her, Sylvia was certain that she would respond and that no account of sexual sensation from a friend or book would ever again gall her. When Han said "goodnight" to his father and turned off the bedroom light, Sylvia toted her physical craving up the steps. She kept an anxious eye on the state of her desire while she undressed and washed in the bathroom.

Pale and pensive, bent over his shoes, Han sat on the edge of the bed. Undoing his tie, his belt, then snapping them off, his vague eyes turned to her and drifted away while he discussed the kinds of music that he would try the following day.

"Dad didn't mind the pain at all, but, damn, it was there." Standing, Han slipped his pants through a hanger. "Want a shirt?" He smiled as he lifted the sheet.

"Just you," she croaked, then blushed at the false sound of her voice.

It was the saddest mystery that the immediate sensations streaming from her flesh to her brain should not amplify, but actually erode the passion that she'd so carefully reinforced with whiskey.

Rocking them with a rueful whistle, kissing her lips and face, Han lay heavily for a moment, then hung above her on stiff arms. "Damn it!" His face slid over her stomach, "Hold on, darling! I won't leave you hanging."

Caught unawares, Sylvia groaned with pleasure at his ardent mouth. Her hips tossed up without a guiding image and flaring with feeling, she moved against his tongue. Then her mind, with its demand for pressure and depth, survived the ambush, peered aghast from the bright ceiling.

Han felt her freeze and glanced up.

"I'm too sensitive now," she tugged his ear. I miss your face. I want to kiss you."

"Do you? Again, then?" Han kissed her forehead. "I love to launch you."

"I love you, Han, and I loved that!"

Pulling up the sheet, Sylvia kissed his face and reached to put out the light. Her drink stood by.

"But you're exhausted, you sweet man. You must sleep,"

Han slipped his hand between her legs, "Tomorrow," he murmured. When he turned on his side and slept, Sylvia sat up in the dark and drank down the large glass of liquor like water. Poking the pillow, she slipped down and felt the heat of his back on the skin of her own. They lay together, a double wall, at peace for the night.

In the morning, Han sleeping peacefully beside her, Sylvia imagined herself in a room as bright as a summer noon. Alison was coughing. Sylvia took the cigarette from her hand and gave it back when the fit had passed. "You're reasonable," said the ironic voice. "I would only have lighted another. "

Sylvia grew weak with her heart's dispatch of thrilled and disbelieving blood. Could it really be so simple, so direct? The woman was just kissing her, saying, "I'm mad to go to bed. Are you?" Her frank, ragged tone tickled Sylvia's gut. "I know what you're feeling. Really, I do. I've been there myself. Oh, put away your fists and just allow me."

That exquisite mouth, there, where she was so ugly? Alison would hate her when she saw.

"No, you are not wood. My god, you're not."

Dark, defensive, Sylvia's legs were a trembling frame for that confident, blond head. "Wounds heal, you know. I'm going to heal you." Glancing up, her eyes were thick with will. "If it takes three days, I'm going to please you. If it takes forever."

"No, no, no!' She would not leave the sunny white room in her mind. She was going to lie in bed for as long as she wanted to and lift up her legs, one at a time, admiring them. The room curved round her like the shell of an egg, from which, when she allowed it, her future would hatch. Furious, deeply angry, her longing to stay there was being swept aside by another force.

"No!" She cried, awake and struggling in Han's grip. He pushed down her wrists with a teasing smile and threw his leg over hers. I want a repeat performance. Last night was great."

"I was dreaming I'd just lost the case. I'm surprised I woke up at all." Laughing, she received his diving body. At first his eagerness seemed a compliment, but hardly had she rejoiced at their restored normalcy when his hard weight struck her as imperious and she doubled her hands into fists on his back. When he left her to take a shower, she still felt the pressure of his body.

In the kitchen, eating the breakfast Han had cooked, her heavy, irritable feeling continued. When Han described the morning temperature as unseasonably warm, Spring almost, Sylvia decided the source of her mood was the freak weather.

"It's the humidity," she told herself to explain the anger his goodbye kiss aroused. Climbing to the street at the courthouse stop, she looked up into the sky at the top of the stairs. The air pressed the steeple cross like a soft balloon which must surely puncture and flood the square with a watery heat.

When the small door opened behind the bench and the judge stepped through, fear took over her, and all morning long her racing heart and brain kept her sense of oppression at bay.

But at lunch, at the restaurant where Harry Rodman always ate when on trial, Sylvia felt that she was filling up with his slow, flat voice, that his laborious review of the morning, and anticipation of the afternoon, was packing her with rage.

Harry Rodman always drank one martini at lunch and now the waitress was taking away the glass. Held high on her tray, it dashed the sun from the window across Sylvia's eyes. For a moment in the stifling restaurant, her hope flowed. When this un-typical weather moved past the city, her dreadful mood would lift. Mrs. Smith would fly home to take charge of her household. Realizing his eccentricity when he saw his mother's shock, Han would bar Doc from the house and, hopefully, end their relationship. Han and Sylvia would move back downtown to her austere apartment and resume their former life.

Heavy with food, Harry Rodman kept yawning as he read the paper. His stretched lips and deep sighs caused Sylvia's closed mouth to ache. But she knew not to yawn in the partner's presence, even with the newspaper between them, and never to drink.

"She's been brought up right," Harry Rodman had croaked to Han that first lunch when she'd ordered a coke. Such grim approval made her grateful for her mother's strict ways and she smugly prided herself on the discipline which kept her as sharp after lunch as she was in the early morning. Her noiseless nocturnal trips to the bathroom where she would gulp from the bottle until she was drunk on her feet were events too rare (although they occurred every night) to count.

The back of Harry Rodman's newspaper didn't interest her. If Han hadn't deserted the case, she'd have joined him in a brief walk after lunch to follow the smells and sounds of the seafront while shivers of excitement passed along her spine. But that was before this inversion, this tomb of wet, polluted, strangling air.

"That damn newspaper," she mentally shrieked. She longed to plunge her forefinger through it repeatedly and rapidly, making air holes so that she could breathe.

CHAPTER 13

"The conquering hero, dad!" Han raised his fist in triumph and waved Sylvia through the door. "She's come to kiss you good night."

Covering his confusion with a sweet smile, Judge Smith made a brushing motion at the chair that stood in her way. Han pushed it against the wall.

"Sylvia won her case today, dad," Han reminded him. "She's come to tell you about it."

"How lovely of you, my dear, to spare some time for a lazy old man." Serenely, he accepted the kiss of a strange young woman and ignored the plunge of his book table as Sylvia backed into it.

"Oh, no! Oh, god!" She lunged at the falling books. "I'm so stupid!" Sylvia despaired as she gathered the books and put them back on the table. "I'm clumsier every day." She rushed to the door.

"I'm sorry!"

"Alison's such a handsome girl, Han." Watching the empty door, the judge spoke softly. "I'm sorry to see her so worked up."

"Three weeks in court is a long time – but she won it." Han jumped in the air and landed lightly on his toes. "The litigation department's going to make its first woman partner. It's great!"

Judge Smith accepted Han's excitement with an affectionate smile.

He looked carefully at the door, put his hand to his mouth and whispered. "I didn't even know Alison had gone to law school. How long has she been in the firm, Han?" He shifted his hand to his ear. "I feel like a damn fool."

"Do you really think that woman is Alison?"

"Who else could it be?" Lifting his hands and brows, his father's cynical hilarity affected Han like a strong drink. It had been four weeks since his mother had left for Phoenix and Han felt that he too had been living in a foreign scene. The daily routine was filtered through his memories of early childhood, wrapping him in a romantic, mysterious, elemental world.

By means of this mental sorcery, even his father's cynicism was tinged with the wonderful. Han's only justification and hope for pardon had been the fact that Alison and Sylvia were too different to be compared. But his father simply merged them both into the magical stereotype of Han's wife. Guilt intensified the hope with which he clung to the protection of this ancestral dodge. What relief to bury Sylvia in "The Wife."

"Alison must be awfully good in court, Han." The judge looked gratefully up at Han as his scheduled shot of charm flowed into him.

"She thinks she was terrible because she wasn't smooth and eloquent, but the impression she gives of constantly fighting off stage fright makes her seem totally honest. She can't accept it, but she's brilliant."

"Are you?"

Checking his father's feet, the gray color of his face, Han smiled. "Am I what?"

"Are you brilliant in court?"

"I don't know yet, dad. Sylvia's been trying the case."

"Your wife's going to shoot ahead," he whimsically smiled. "You'd better get back."

"Can a career compare with a good book?"

"Nice boy, smart boy. I was so impressed by those articles you wrote in school. I'd like to read them again. I remember one piece in particular you wrote for the *Law Review* – defending bussing. Would you dig that out of my file?"

Han turned out the lamps and stepped back with a teasing smile.

"You're losing your grip, dad. You thought I was a lousy writer."

"Nonsense. Not at all."

"I remember having to defend that Review article line by line. You were furious. You said it was garbage, badly reasoned, poorly expressed."

"Ridiculous! You were just sensitive, as all students are. You'd understand the admiration behind what I said if we had the same discussion now."

Han flew down the stairs with the dinner tray. In the hall mirror, as he quickly passed, he saw the dining room chandelier and Sylvia beneath it, bowed over her legal pad at the dining room table.

"You' re so sweet. But I'm angry with you for washing up your victory dinner."

Han kissed the top of her head. Her thick soft curls were a barrier to her neck, then a refuge from the cold surface that his lips found. Filling his hands with her hair, he straightened and lightly tugged.

"My father thinks I'm a good writer."

"How nice," she murmured as she wrote. "I'm glad."

Han laughed at her cordial, distracted tone and made reins of her hair.

"How would you describe that?" Sylvia pointed across the table. She was making an inventory of the furniture.

"What? The low boy? That's early 17th century American, Philadelphia. Why bother about it? Much too big for Doc to snitch." Sitting down beside her, sliding his elbow in a luxurious spread across the glowing table, he propped his head in his hand and grinned up at her disapproving face. "What do you care, tonight? You've won the case." He tapped her wrist. "Do you realize that? You won it! Don't continue this absurdity tonight. Drink! Drink more! Be happy!"

"I'm a successful tactic, that's all. You told me what to say and I said it. You really won that case and don't think Harry Rodman doesn't know it."

Still buoyant with his father's praise, Han quietly accepted her gloom and made them drinks in the pantry. He came singing back to her side. She sipped primly and frowned up at him.

"Why are you so happy?"

"I'm proud of you – you darling! The jury believed you."

Suspicion darkened Sylvia's face.

"If I was jealous of you, Sylvia, do you think – good god, you're stupid!"

Smiling at this tardy truth, Sylvia grabbed his hand.

"You've no reason to be happy. That's why I don't believe you. You've done yourself irreparable damage at the office! And your mother won't come back. It's ghastly!"

"Every time mother calls, I urge her to stay. I don't want to go back to work."

She was alarmed. "But why?"

"I'm happy! He brought his hands between them and turned up his palms. "I'm happy!"

"You have no reason to be." Obdurately, she continued her prissy tone.

"If I needed a reason, I wouldn't be happy. Look at you!"

"You're right." She whispered with shocking fear. "Look at me."

Han suddenly recognized the wooden body that he'd recently felt when they made love. Thick and dull in her eyes and flesh – surely, she must be ill. There was some fear deeper than the tension of the trial that she both suffered and denied. He touched her dry lips.

"What's the matter?"

"I'm not a valid person," she whispered, "I don't work. "

"You work too hard. You don't have to work with me. I understand ascetic moods. Everyone has them."

"Not me." Tossing her head, she challenged him with a cocky look. "That's not my problem. I can't get enough."

"In the last two weeks or so, you've been pushing yourself with me, am I wrong?" He retreated from her alarm. "I am wrong then. I know I've kept you hanging, or so I thought. "

"But you haven't."

"You looked so frightened when you said you weren't a valid person."

"I'm scared witless," she yelled, "but not about sex. I'm just so jealous of you!"

"At the firm? What are you talking about? We're going in opposite directions."

"And you – you don't even care. You're not fighting. You want me to replace you, yet you're even prepping me to take your place."

"Come on, Sylvia. Just until mother gets home."

"You're not competitive anymore. I'm so jealous!"

"But you want to race. You've always said so."

"I thought it was the only thing to do. I thought that dropouts, carpenters, housewives, were all lying about the *rat race* because for some reason they'd been bumped off course. I was so sure it was worth all the crap, because it's the most respected way – and everybody knows it. But you just slowed down. It's worse than happy – you're enchanted."

"I haven't done anything to you, Sylvia." Palms up, Han teasingly pleaded. "You act as though I'd stolen something from you."

To his astonishment she accused him more ardently than ever.

"You were born King of the Mountain. You were born smart and good looking. You were born rich. It's not fair!"

"Aren't you naturally endowed? Your brilliance, your good looks?" He held out his arms, dropping them slowly at her look of stony resentment. "It's true, you had to work harder, but you can see how I'm trying to equalize us – and you don't approve?"

"You dare to." Sylvia rapped the table, "Harry Rodman's awed by you and so is that corrupt Doc, although that doesn't stop him from robbing you blind. He's selling you dog piss and cocaine for your fortune. He's stealing all the important silver in this house and yet you respect – holy hell! – you *love* him!"

"To them that hath shall be given."

Sylvia thrust her face close to his. "It stinks!"

Turning from her bitter smile, Han, quiet now, took her hand, pressing hard against the chill in her fingers.

"The bonnie boy is depressed for a change? Oh, dear!" She taunted.

Slowly, he pushed her fingers back until, with a shriek, she yanked her hand away.

"I wish I'd broken a few," he smiled as she gripped her fingers. "Stop degrading yourself and quit that damned furniture inventory. It's pathetic to be so concerned about other people's property. It's what keeps women down, this clerking for the rich. Why do you do it?" He tried to grab her pen, then tore the corner of the long yellow page she'd been writing on. "If I don't care, why should you? It's only to ease your own bourgeois conscience that you're trying to help my mother."

Sylvia defended herself with disdain.

"When she comes home to a bunch of bare rooms, I hope she'll be somewhat comforted to know exactly what was stolen and when. With this!" She waved the yellow sheet, "she'll be able to rush to the Insurance Company before she unpacks." Shaking her head, Sylvia stared across the table, then gripped her brow and groaned.

"How can you let him get away with it? That beautiful silver candlestick."

"I asked Doc twice because you're so upset. He says he didn't take it."

"He's lying," she agonized. "Don't you know that?"

"Oh, so what. I believe what he says."

"Certainly, you do." Han's boredom over the matter incensed her. "Because if Doc is looting this house, it might really be dog piss and cocaine that's going into your father's veins and you certainly can't afford to think that."

"Most certainly not." He laughed.

"You're wicked!"

"Wicked?" He gently pinched her nose

"It's so indulgent, so decadent," she fumed. "But you'll pay for it tomorrow. Tomorrow's Friday. Oh yes. It's Friday and I'm going to wipe you off the tennis court."

"You always do. You've licked me the last six Fridays straight."

"Not really," she gloomed.

Han dug in his jacket for his appointment book. "Take a look at the scores, killer. Take a good look and have a drink.

CHAPTER 14

"You said I could beat you!"

Tossing her a ball, Han quailed before Sylvia's dense disappointment. As she walked to the baseline, her betrayed back roused him to a fever of justification.

"Come on, Sylvia! You've been beating me steadily. This is the first good night I've had for six weeks. I'm not playing well."

"It's just that you're off. You're hitting too hard, like I used to."

"Why don't we just rally?"

"Certainly, it's your game Han." She smoldered. "You never lose anything."

When they'd dressed and were out on the street, Sylvia looked so miserable that he was almost afraid to suggest their customary stop in the neighborhood tavern for a drink. When she hauled open the bar door and headed for their usual place, Han found himself on tiptoe behind her. He remained ruefully cautious as he smoked and drank, seeing that his routine gestures were salt in her mysterious wound. Han had never known her to get drunk in public but tonight she fueled her sulkiness with swift shots of scotch until he shrank from her.

"You promised I could beat you." Her lower lip poked out in blatant regression as he paid the bill. Leading her along the streets to his father's house, Han felt himself to be in the possession of a gigantic infant.

"You promised you'd make love to me." Mortified that his father might be listening below, Han strained against the grip of her hands and closed the bedroom door.

His dread grew as he felt the inertness of Sylvia's mouth and skin. Her passionate words and noises were confusing and frightening.

"No!" She cried as he lifted away.

Sylvia placed her feet on either side of his waist. She took his hands and thrust him towards the ceiling. Suspended above her on the four supports of her dark, strong limbs, Han laughed in spite of himself.

"Deactivated" Sylvia finally declared and, dipping her knees, shot him over the footboard. He tucked up his legs to miss the dresser and landed on the floor by the bed.

"Very nice." Laconically, she approved, as though watching a lovelorn stunt.

Yanking Sylvia off the bed, Han pressed down her shoulders with his knees. He got one wrist to the floor and was struggling to catch her other hand when she unseated him with a toss of her hips. Supported on her elbows, Sylvia waited calmly for his next attack. In the intense struggle, her body was light again and warm. She was strong, agile and mean.

"Quit!" He cried. "I've got a cramp," He struggled off her and reached for his leg.

"Grab my leg," he yelled, "I can't stand it. Dig into the muscle. Dig into me! I'm in agony!" He gave her a desperate shove.

"Where were you at the Battle of Armageddon?" She sneered. "What a wonderful lover: 'I've got a cramp, mommy' God, how dumb. 'Help me, mom!' Moron! I could feel you. I was normal!'"

Then she suddenly became morose.

"Well, not really. I'd give anyone a cramp. You're not really a moron, you're just swimming in the Bering Straits. You should go back to Alison, back to the normal. If I ever say I hate you – it's me I hate. Even a cramping moron should be able to figure that out. God damn the that cramp!" Sylvia swooshed flat on the bed.

Fascinated, stubborn, Han knelt at the bedside and swept apart her lovely legs. Was there something wrong with her? The dryness, her stillness. First light, then heavy; teasing, then blunt, he worked and worked. Raising his head, he eased his knees on the bare floor and sought again the center of her sensation. When she began to toss and groan, he attacked in a last surge of tiredness and pain, then clung while she tossed until her energy reversed and she was frantically clutching him.

Drawn up her body like a quilt, he loved her strength and the touch of her hands as she sculpted his flesh. Rocking him, stroking him, praising him, he felt his fatigue change to valor – until she breathed one word that threw him.

"Did you say *Alison*?" He asked sharply, raising his face from hers.

"Alison." The sound of his wife's name, blurry with drink and sentiment, formed on Sylvia's lips.

"Alison?" He repeated. "Why?"

"Alison." Sylvia's whisper, adoring and bizarre, sank him into sleep.

It was a bright, mild morning but Sylvia woke in a tomb of woe; Han could see that his zest was a torment to her. Joke and tease as he might, her hangover distressed her, and he couldn't dispatch Sylvia's anxious preoccupation. Although she ate breakfast in a generous square of sun formed by the kitchen window, she begged for a sweater and even then, she sat outside and nibbled in a clutch of cold. When he finished with his father and stepped out on the terrace to join her, he felt the pull of her mood through the sunny air.

"Want a beer?" Han felt he was speaking into a cave.

"A beer?" She despaired. "My god, I need so much more than a beer! It's so messed up. I'm messed up! How can you stand it? Go back to Alison."

"Don't say that," he pleaded.

"Don't want the slut taking liberties with the sacred name." Sylvia mimicked his expression for a second then drooped with shame.

"I never, *never* compare Alison and you. You're so different! You are the opposite of Alison and she is the opposite of you. Comparison is impossible!"

"Of course it is. She's beautiful, charming, and intelligent," Sylvia said with withering masochism. "The normal woman. The normal marriage. Wait!"

Pressing her hand to his mouth she said with sincerity, "If I could give up eternity for normalcy, I wouldn't hesitate. I'm in love with your life with Alison. A farmhouse in a country town. Two attractive sons. The husband commutes to an important job while the wife sees to their social life and really works on the children. Really works, because in so many ways, intellectually, morally, athletically, they've got to be first rate. Saturday nights are a celebration. Humorous couples drive over from the next hamlet. There's steak or fish on a barbecue, lots of drinks, lots of children booming around, dogs, loud music, dancing and jokes and when the party's over and the mess is cleared up, there's a ferocious renewal of attraction in the master bedroom. That's normalcy."

"It didn't seem quite like that – living it." Han stepped over to the fish pool. The brick backs of the identical houses were reflected with the sky and clouds on the surface of the pool. As he leaned over, the picture of his face entered the complexity. Standing across from him the dark curly top of Sylvia's head narrowly overlapped the yellow curve of his hair.

"Did I make it sound like that? I didn't mean to." He spoke to Sylvia's image. "So much has happened. I can't go back!" Han saw the intensity of her shock; his mouth was stone when he tried to smile.

"She'll forgive you, Han. She's a wonderful woman."

"The dim, cold rooms. On Sundays, the desolate noon sun. 'I have my chores. You have yours'."

"She didn't lose her dignity. You leave, come back, the children haven't missed a day of school, the house is always clean. She won't be hard on you."

"She's marvelous, Alison," Han agreed, filling up with dread.

"Those kids won't run wild – not with her! 'Where've you been?' she'll say when you walk in the door. She'll look up from whatever she's doing and cough like hell from her cigarette. Alison can take care of everything. What's your little vacation to her? You're married to a noble woman."

Sylvia stepped around the pool and took his arm. "If we were married and you had an affair, I'd be moribund with jealousy, but Alison copes. She's so incredible! She must be her own ideal."

"Oh, she is!" In a nose-dive of depression as Sylvia stopped speaking, Han could only whisper. How could he explain how Alison had disappointed him a thousand times. 'It's lovely today, very mild. The boys are out on the river. You won't believe the steak the butcher saved for me. I bought two bottles of the wine you liked last Saturday. I can't wait to see you!'

On the train home, the house still ahead, his excitement was an exquisite tug.

Then, at the house, the reality would kick in. Those dim, cold rooms, those ragged boys. "Peter won't take out the garbage. That broken glass is Freddy's work. You've got to punish them.'"

Alison's greeting kiss – thrust-out chin, the bang of her cheek on his mouth, then – 'the damn furnace has gone berserk, can you fix it?'

He always fixed it. So many times the disappointment, so many times.

"Did you love taking the train home every night? Wasn't it magical?"

Staring into the fish pool as Sylvia spoke, Han took her hand. Two houses shining in the water, two heads. When reading to his father the previous week, he had learned that the location of sight is deep inside the head. Like a moviegoer, the consciousness sits with its back to the eyes to watch the display in the brain. Contrary to sensation, he was not at the edge of his mind making sense of what he saw, but, at the last point in a long construction of significance, buried in his brain.

"There is an outside," he stretched out his hands, "but the meaning is all in the brain." Han dropped to his knees and leaned out over the pool. Still the two houses were playfully fused. Sylvia's face overlapped his, yet a thousand images of Alison tracked along the spongy surface of his brain. In anguish, Han stretched his hands wide and plunged them into the pool.

"Your theory?" Sylvia respectfully asked.

Han watched the leaping shapes and forms with delight. "Demolition," he murmured and when the water smoothed down, he moved the forefinger of each hand in quick unison. Two circles of waves sped towards each other and passed through to break at each end of the pool.

"Are you demonstrating your theory?" Sylvia asked.

Han concentrated on the synchronization of the two circles of spreading waves, varying the number and rate that formed from his hands until, crests falling into troughs, the houses in the pool and the two heads blinked blank. As if the discharge of his mental tension was a propellant, for a few seconds Han felt he was floating over the fish pool. The return to weight and confusion as his image popped back was torture. A prison in the desolate noon sun. *I have my chores, you have yours*, Han crashed into Sylvia as he jumped up. Turning around, he hugged her hard.

"Tell me about weekends in the country, Han."

The dutiful feeling of her arms around his neck, her dreamy voice and the cool smell of her skin made him happy. Taking her hand, he led her to the deck chairs by the kitchen door.

"Make it normal," she settled down. "No flights of fancy like the last time when you told me the boys dug a huge hole under the apple tree because you told them there was treasure buried there, I hate fairytales!" Her legs bounced petulantly on the long stretch of chair. "I want a typical Saturday morning."

"That was typical – perfectly normal."

"Come on! That's one of the nastiest things I've ever heard."

"It was a joke. I never thought the boys would believe me. Alison and I had the laugh of our lives when we saw that pit – that crater."

"Alison would never be so cruel! "

"I was the one who told them." He winced at the memory.

"She never would have laughed. Neither would you," she added, from fairness, not concern. "Normal parents aren't monsters. You know what I like to hear about. The kind of Saturday morning when Alison goes off to play tennis and you take the boys into the village to spend their allowances and get haircuts."

Han glanced at the corner of the yard where he'd shoveled for buried treasure in a fever of excitement. How could that have happened? The same trick his father had pulled on him! He'd laughed off the boys' frantic indignation, called them "sore heads". He and Alison had actually worried that their lack of humor would put them at a disadvantage as they went on in life. When he'd told the story of the buried treasure, Doc's broad hand had measured the height of an eight-year-old boy. In the next generation Freddy had been eight and Peter ten. Where in hell between the two childhoods had his memory gone? Was his father an amnesiac also?

Han bobbed up and swung his feet between the two chairs.

"One Saturday, I took the kids to town. Peter bolted his coke and threw up all over the counter," Sylvia flipped a disgusted hand.

"Too dramatic."

"But it happened,"

"Once," she sniffed, "I want the usual."

Han leaned over her legs and felt the heat of her white trousers on his face as he described the front lawn in winter, stretching snow-smooth down to the river.

"It was the worst blizzard I remember." He paused for her censorship of the uncommon, but Sylvia was absorbed. "The boys hauled the snow shoes out of the cellar. Alison had a fit at the dirt in the kitchen and when we first set off, we left grids of dirt in the snow. The boys loved it. They got more excited seeing tracks than when they spotted the deer or raccoon that left them. I suppose they felt like trappers."

He laughed at her warning eyes and put his mind on the action. The memory of that snowy afternoon, the trek to the pine grove and the beaver dam and the clap of sunset that met them on their return at the edge of the woods covered the reality of his domestic life like the thin ice that topped the river.

"Did the Hardins bring over their kids?" Sylvia relished the predictability of the Pleasantville routine.

"Brought the scotch over too. Tinker got in a foul mood because her husband couldn't take his eyes off Alison."

"Well, she's so beautiful."

"Oh, she was."

"SHE IS!".

"She's a tyrant, you fool. I *hate* her!"

It was the most intense emotional admission of his life and Sylvia shot up with him, radiantly relieved. Down again, ill with disloyalty, Han sought her chastisement.

"I don't hate her because I love you!"

"Certainly not."

He kept smiling into her somber gaze. "You can't compare two perfect things. It's not knocking winter to love spring."

For once Sylvia laughed as wildly as he. "You've got to see her today, Han. She'll understand everything, if you just tell her. You'll be back before dinner if you start now. I'll drive out with you. I can stay in the car while you have your talk."

CHAPTER 15

As they drove North out of the city, Han asked himself why he was following Sylvia's directions like a robot. 'Call the agency,' she'd ordered, 'and get an aide to take charge of your father!' Meanwhile Han would seek forgiveness from Alison. Why was he driving his mother's car when her iron law forbade no other driver but herself? The idea of it all was making him nauseous with anxiety. As soon as he had a chance, he pulled over.

"Swop places with me, Sylvia," he croaked. "Please."

Sylvia stared calmly at Han's face and walked around to take the wheel. Her startled glance made Han look in the mirror. His skin was wet and ashy.

"It's all this gray," he gestured feebly at the roof and seats. "It's mother's favorite color.'"

Sylvia's childish laugh, loud and boisterous, betrayed her excitement in her role as driver. The tips of her fingers seemed in loving contact with the wheel. Her eyes lifted constantly to the rear-view mirror while she pressed to go faster than the cluster of surrounding cars. She flicked him a roguish glance as she passed out a truck or car. She answered horns with a thrust of her chin.

"I suddenly know why I'm working," she briefly gripped his knee. 'This beautiful car! I've got to have one! I don't care how much. It's the very first *big* thing that I'm going to buy."

"Doc would approve of you. You enjoy the loot."

She smiled.

"The steel, the rubber, the ivory ..." Han touched the glossy dashboard. "It's all stolen."

"Oh, really?" Sylvia's glance was tart. "Give Doc one more month and single handed he'll have redressed the balance." She tapped the steering wheel. "I'll die if he runs off with this."

Driving to the edge of the city, the heavy gray car seemed to Sylvia the source of all motion – the humming center of a vast disc – buildings, people, cars in a dense whirl. Moving slower or faster as Sylvia braked or gunned, the car was gaily obedient. What did will or desire have to do with a velocity imposed from without? Or within?

But as the car entered the tunnel that plunged under the river, Han felt dense with passivity. It was a struggle to dig the card out of his pocket for the toll.

"Pleasantville," Sylvia cried. Now it was the countryside on either side of the highway that was the engine of their speed.

When the road put the sun directly on the windshield Han blinked rapidly and yawned while Sylvia shadowed her acute gaze with her hand.

"Ignore the first three signs and take Route 67."

The turn of her wrist yanked the sun from his eyes, slid him across the seat and held him helpless against her side as the narrow exit swirled them round its circle. Released at the intersection, Han returned to the passenger seat without complaint or surprise. In the long, bronze beam of the setting sun, Sylvia's eyes slid over the gilded country scene.

"There's the Post Office," she cried. "We go right, then over the bridge at the end of the town. I wonder how I know? These wonderful old houses: I've never seen such imperial trees. Listen!" She exulted as the planks of the old wooden bridge rumbled under the wheels of the car.

The road ran for three miles beside the river and then to Sylvia's intense excitement, patches of fields and woods pushed the glimmer of water to a friendly distance.

"I *knew* the river would be on the right."

The handsome, varied houses that they passed were only interesting to Han as a test of Sylvia's intuition. Tucked among flowering bushes, guarded by handsome stone walls, graceful in their slow decay, none fit the demands of her imagination. But when she saw an old brick wall and gatepost in the dense grip of ivy and honeysuckle, she indicated and turned before Han spoke.

"Why does this seem so familiar, Han? This narrow dirt road is like a magical tunnel through the woods. I go left, here!" She turned at a fork in the dirt road before he could speak. "I don't believe in reincarnation," Sylvia glowed with excitement. "But the feeling of familiarity is just so strong."

"Look at the weeds," Han stared dismally. "Damn those boys! It's a disgrace!"

"Holy hell," Sylvia grinned at him. "You've aged half a lifetime. What a voice! You look so stern!"

Poison ivy had spread everywhere through the light growth of the woods and Han felt his chest and stomach tighten with his old irritation. That ivy should have been burned out by now. Why wasn't Alison on top of the boys? Christ! If this was a preview of how things had been going, he'd be working like a robot all spring and summer. His hands angrily slammed the dashboard as Sylvia stopped the car.

Vigorous trees on either side of the driveway presented the farmhouse beneath the arch of their branches.

"Every damn branch that I cut back last summer is sprouting," Han snarled at the crowding trees. "You should have seen how nice I made it look. In the rear-view mirror when I'd leave in the morning it all looked especially romantic." He rapped the mirror in despair. "That picture stays with me all day and I forget that the great dinner and the wine won't happen because it always takes so long to unclog the toilet or put down the strip of floor and Alison can't help falling asleep – but what the hell," he checked his rage, "that's life, isn't it?"

Sylvia reacted to his desolation as though criticized. "It is normal! You shouldn't be living in a huge old country house if you don't want to be handy. You can't expect Alison to do it all. Oh, no!" She cried, blushing at his sneer. "You're the same way about the firm – which is just normal working life. You've got to come to terms with normalcy, Han."

When he got out, Sylvia leaned over and pulled the passenger door closed.

"Don't leave me!" Han cried.

Sylvia closed the car door and looked at him. "You don't want Alison and the boys to see me. I'll just explore until you come back."

His rage at her stupidity didn't flare, but fell back on him instead. Under its weight the only possible movement was a sinking down. He crossed his arms on his chest and blinked rapidly into the setting sun. "I'm a black hole," he murmured, getting back in the car.

She started the engine and looked around. "I don't see anywhere to turn. I can't back up all that way. Oh, shit! Are you ill? What is it?" She drove towards the house, "I'll turn around fast. If anyone notices, I'll yell out the window that I'm lost, you duck."

"It's okay, drive up," Han directed. "The car's gone," he pointed to the lean-to. "But what the hell has happened?"

Han was confused. Squinting against the sun, he raised his eyebrows, puzzled. Was it possible that the evergreen tree, its roots tugged from the ground, was lying along the roof of the house? Fending off the sun as they left the woods, Han strained to see.

They stared at the house as they got out of the car. It lay under the ancient dead tree, which had crashed right through the roof.

"How truly weird!" Sylvia said as she followed him around the corner of the house.

Han rattled the knob of the back door then stepped behind the lilac bush and looked in the kitchen window. "Can't see anything."

He held back a branch as she followed. "The sun's pouring through the house, into my face."

Hunched and quiet, she stepped up beside him and looked through the dining room window. Beneath its new and novel ceiling of pine boughs, the pretty maple dining table was bright as the river in the late afternoon sun. The four chairs were drawn up at the exact intervals that Alison unfailingly insisted on and their look of serene acceptance of the punctured roof above made Han howl with laughter.

"How fares your sense of the familiar now?"

He kept stopping to look back as he followed Sylvia to the car. His hilarity as he speculated on what must have occurred kept erupting from him with the force of those puncturing boughs. The huge tree had been dead for years, and in the wind of some autumn storm, must have cracked and fallen on the house. Those thick branches plunging through the roof he'd put on, the ceiling he'd plastered and painted, the floors he'd repeatedly scraped and stained and polished – again and again this track of destruction sent his mind reeling. Sylvia's stolid face only prolonged his fit as he laughed.

"They're gone, not dead," he kept explaining to Sylvia as she worried about Alison and the children. "If they were dead the car would be under the lean-to. How could Alison have locked the kitchen door if she'd been impaled?"

"You' re awful!"

"You don't understand suburban life," Han said. For the next week the tree's imagined fall delighted him.

After her victory, Harry Rodman wanted Sylvia on all his cases. Her working day was exhausting and late at night, when Han fixed her a sandwich and poured them each a drink, her doleful silence came across as reproach.

The memory of their shared elation in the garden when

he'd admitted to hating Alison gave him hope that she was but temporarily punishing them both.

Sylvia was so done in by Friday that he sought to put off the tennis.

"Fat chance!" She'd countered. "Tonight's going to be my comeback."

But she really wasn't up for the game. Any ball that wasn't right at her feet was a cruelty. Surprisingly slow, almost sluggish, it distressed Han to watch her run.

Finally, she threw down her racket. "I'm crying for Alison," she stormed. "You don't know if she's dead or not. But what's really so terrible is that all this time she's been gone! I haven't been able to help her."

On Saturday morning his aching muscles reminded him that before he'd been able to arouse Sylvia's sexual energy, she'd broken away and curled up, sobbing over Alison. On Sunday when he suggested the telling of a few Pleasantville stories, the rueful retreat of her eyes criticized him, and his defenses dropped before the sincerity of her grief.

"Just normalcy?" He gently smiled.

"I feel awful!" Her legs trembled in the warm sun.

"Look," he sat by her feet. "There are many things I've never told you." He stroked her hair. "When you're re-reading your favorite books don't you love being back before all the horrors begin, before the bad marriage, or the pathetic death, or the war or the financial disaster?"

"All that made-up junk! You told me Pleasantville was absolutely real!"

"It is."

"It's gone."

In his mind, Han saw the tree falling, but dared not laugh lest he arouse Sylvia's dismay at his cruelty. Staring at her, he took long, numbing breaths.

CHAPTER 16

"Shut up, idiot!" Sylvia growled at the frightened whine that had been in her head all day. Standing on a subway platform holding onto a post, Sylvia leaned out over the track to look for the uptown train. "But I am happy!" She scolded the tiny anxious voice prompted by Han's comment at breakfast that morning. He'd wondered what could make her happy these days.

"Why should a fried egg on a freaky hot day make me happy?" She'd responded. "Look at that sky out there!" Pushing away her plate, she'd grabbed the cereal box and held up the last silver spoon against the murky light.

"It's so disgraceful, your indulgence. Doc praises you for being *happy* as though you were especially endowed to achieve the only aim of life. Praising you for your faith, he picks you clean and turns your father into a dope addict. God, you're such a baby, such a fool!"

Graceful and solid as he leaned against the kitchen counter, Han had turned his amused face from her to the intercom at the eruption of his father's furious voice.

"The next step is heroin Han, and even you can't afford much of that."

Han kissed her forehead and went whistling from the kitchen. "Sore head," he called back. "See you tonight."

How she resented his sympathy. "There's nothing wrong with me! I'm overworked and it's too damn hot!"

Later, on her way home from work, those thoughts returned with the howl of the uptown train. As they entered a tunnel, Sylvia stood back as two amiable Latina women stepped into the car. She admired their cheer as they hung onto their pocketbooks and endured the strain and drama of the jolting, wailing ride. Coming and going, just to stick to one's body through the thousands of days was first class work, she thought. What was happiness compared to endurance?

"I am a very happy person!" But as soon she emerged into the street once more uptown, her anxious voice began again.

"When I walk through Battery Park, I love the smell of cut grass. I love that yellow ball of sun. When the wind shifts, the harbor smells wonderful and Harry Rodman's really beginning to trust me…"

Her reverie was shattered suddenly by a boy racing round the street corner at high velocity, sneakers slapping the ground. Oh, trouble! Oddly, he looked like one of Han's sons. He brushed into Sylvia as he swept past her, and she tottered on her feet.

"Sorry!" He yelled. "Didn't mean to hit you!"

Outside a neighborhood bar, he shouted again.

"Come home with me, mother. That place stinks! It stinks in there!"

As a woman emerged from the bar swearing and raised her fist at the boy, Sylvia thought of the ruined Pleasantville house and recognized none other than Han's wife. Alison loped unsteadily towards the corner.

"Alison, wait!" Sylvia approached, and kept her balance as Alison grabbed her hand, shaking.

"You know me," said Sylvia. "The bar. We sat on the churchyard wall."

"I know liquor's been taking me out these days, but a churchyard wall?"

"You know me." Sylvia tried to smile.

"That's stark. Now don't look so hurt. There's a shred coming back… We had a fine talk in that blue door bar one night and we parted the best of friends. Atrocious! Come to my house and have a nightcap. I'm sure it will all come back."

At the street before the one where Sylvia currently lived with Han, Alison led her off the avenue. Two houses up from the corner, Alison climbed steps identical to the ones that Sylvia climbed every evening and unlocked an identical door. Could this be the house that connected to its twin by an underground tunnel?

As Sylvia walked in, she smelled new carpeting and paint and when Alison switched on a light the glare of white space revealed rooms that were replicas of the ones across the yard. There was no stove or refrigerator in the kitchen and the front hall was littered with sawhorses and metal toolboxes. Large squares of sheet rock leaned against the handsome wooden doorways.

"We're still under construction here." Alison stepped into a room that mirrored the one in the house where Han's father lay sick, a fortress of thick drapes and heavy furniture. How could bare walls, a light rug and a narrow wooden platform for a bed so alter her impression of height and depth? And turn a fortress into what? Sylvia shivered.

In the kitchen, there was a vague sour smell, like rotten vegetables. At the sound of her son coming into the hallway behind her, Alison suddenly snapped.

"Why don't you do your damn job!" She shouted at the child.

"I took out the garbage all last week! It's Peter's turn."

She walked back into the hall and began to climb the stairs.

"You can't wake him, Mom." His calm voice drew Alison back down into the hall.

"You can't wake him. He's only been asleep twenty minutes."

"Well, he didn't do his job."

"You'll waste that pill you gave him, and no one will sleep tonight."

"Those awful nightmares," Alison frowned. "What pill? I didn't give Peter a pill tonight."

Freddy picked up a bottle of pills from the counter and brought them to Alison. She hung her head and whispered: "We certainly don't want another night like last night. No, we don't. Oh, no!"

Alison stepped back into the kitchen and Sylvia followed her as she searched around for something, then gazed to the top shelf of the cupboard.

"God, how that boy messes up day after day. Look! There's the booze! Up there! Does he think I'm a damn mountain climber?" Sylvia reached up and handed down the whiskey.

" You!" She exclaimed. "You're tall. Oh, say! You might be just tall enough."

Beckoning Sylvia back into her bedroom, she pushed open a sliding door.

"The ladder's in the cellar and I didn't remember to get it brought up. Would you mind hoisting up these five boxes? It's just wool, very loosely packed. It's so damned annoying, these packets of wool, always under my feet," she crooned as Sylvia stooped and dug her hands under a box. "Push it to the end. Another inch? Good girl! Now, the other boxes will all fit. What wonderful relief! Now, back to the kitchen for your reward."

As the pair sat down at the kitchen table, Sylvia asked, "So, you moved back into town after the tree fell?"

"Yes. Freddy and I had been down at the river pulling the boat out and were soaked through with all that hot, heavy hurricane rain. We were peeling off our clothes, when we heard this mighty bang on the ceiling and saw the most incredible sight. This tree branch stabbing through the plaster, coming down, crashing past us, stabbing through the dining room ceiling."

Alison pushed one glass along the counter, raised her brows and continued her account. "The minute I heard Peter upstairs yelling in a panic, and I knew he hadn't been hurt, I howled with laughter.

Freddy and I fell about, hugging each other, shrieking – even though I knew perfectly well that the insurance wasn't in my name."

Alison waited for the expected response. "All my friends have humor. Please!"

"I don't see the humor in it."

"'Well, drink up and see some!"

Mechanically obedient, Sylvia reached for her glass. She obeyed like a machine because that was the difference between Alison and herself, between life and the mechanical imitations of living that she forced from her body every minute of the day.

"It's so sad!" Sylvia drank and relished Han's laughter, now Alison's, the laughter of happy warriors. If she lived for a hundred years, she could never be like them. But what was the point of loving what she could never be?

"Oh, pooh!" Alison quipped. "Is a storm sad? You should have seen it – the branch stabbing through the ceiling, Freddy's gaping face, Peter's less-than-with-it voice – 'What's going on? What's happening down there?' Lord! I have laughter stored up for years!"

"I don't," Sylvia gloomed, half to herself. "I have mother."

Alison ignored this, laughing again. "*What's going on down there?*"

Suddenly, Alison's mimicry of her son's stupefaction yanked a laugh out of Sylvia. "I'm only imitating," she thought, as breath after breath fueled her whooping mirth.

Alison grabbed the whiskey bottle, put a cigarette in her mouth, plucked up her glass and snapped off the light switch with her elbow.

Sylvia admired the marble mantel in the drawing room as Alison settled on a solid, elegant couch. She sat cross-legged on the rug and poked her knees under a low table. Bending, she sniffed the dark wood.

"She thinks a table is wonderful because of its smell? Innocent creature! To me it's price. What I can get for it. That's well done, but factory made," a quick lift of her upper lip dismissed one sturdy piece. "But only worth the labor of taking it out of here. There's a great deal of interest in redoing houses now. Someone would really dig into their pockets for the paneling in this room and that fireplace would take care of the Pleasantville taxes."

Dreading to discover, Sylvia asked: "That silver candlestick I saw in the kitchen, isn't that worth a fortune?" She waited with dismay as Alison's calculation gave her a peculiar look of laconic greed.

"Sentimental value only. Couple of hundred. It was mother's. Silver doesn't go for much these days, really nothing compared to marble." Alison pointed with the bottle: "I'll rip it out if I have to." She stretched to fill Sylvia's glass. "It's drink up to fill up, you know."

"Did you love your mother?" Sylvia asked with intense relief. The candlestick had not been stolen from the house across the yard.

"Frankly, I was happy when my parents died. But my poor, dear, adoring ex-husband Han—my God, what will he do?"

"Why did he leave you?"

"Why? Why? I made up a story for the boys, shall I make one up for you? You can't be comfortable on that thin rug; come sit by me."

Beguiled, yet afraid of Alison's teasing warmth, Sylvia settled herself on the rug. "I'm fine, thank you."

"The boys think their father fell in love with his secretary because they say they've seen him with a person who looks like a secretary."

Holy hell, that look of fury! Alison knew exactly who she was and was playing a wily game. The snobbish insult was a transforming spell. In a thrice Sylvia was wearing her mother's armor, and sat with her head helplessly bowed.

"Asleep?" Alison asked with soft hostility.

Sylvia forced up her eyes. "It's just so sad."

"Phooey!" Alison rang her glass with her thumbnail. "My husband missed the last train and got a room in a hotel by the harbor. He liked the fog horns at night and the scrambled eggs in the morning, so he decided to stay another night. Days went by, then weeks, then months, but he wasn't deserting his wife and children, he was only staying one more night, only having one more wonderful breakfast at your charming apartment."

"That's no reason," Sylvia whispered.

"Oh, really? How so? If you're bone loyal as Han is and bone bored, the only reasons available are fog horns and moist eggs. You look just like the boys, so sweetly confused, but can't you see that I'm describing an honorable man?"

"Who ran out on you."

"And ducks fly south in the winter," Alison's weathered face was kind again. "Just another way of saying, don't you see, that life isn't personal." Alison poured more whiskey in her glass, then in Sylvia's. She sat back on the couch and pointed with the bottle.

"Don't be so cautious. You'll need another mouthful or two to celebrate my insight, which is," she relit her cigarette, "that there is no choosing. We're swept!" Her freckled hand flashed out. "We're swept and we crash or stagnate and for all the hundreds of reasons why or how, what possibly could have been different when one looks back?" Alison's warm smile was protective. "If one could not have done things differently, then how is it possible not to be just as we are?"

"I've always chosen carefully."

"Worried, you mean. Fretted. And then only afterwards. Buying a dress or a house, setting your cap for a man – I think."

"My life has always followed my mind."

"Phooey! Think of the last time you fell in love."

"I didn't fall in love, I allowed myself to be in love." Sylvia remembered the click of her imperative heels on the marble floor of her office building, when rushing after Han, her feet were as fast as her pounding heart.

"Fiddlesticks!" As though Alison's goal in drinking was to become an elderly woman, liquor was again aging her fast. Handsome, humorous, the admiration of her gaze was the ultimate endorsement of worth, a blue ribbon, a silver cup.

"If there's no choosing, there's no blame." Kicking up her leg, Alison gave it a congenial nod. "God, I'm done with blame."

Sylvia burst out: "If it was impossible to change, then pain would have no purpose!" In her mind, to become a pair of happy warriors was the goal of her race. "It's possible to become!"

"Become? Become what?"

"You."

The white walls glowed as they did in her nightly fantasies, and her yearning eyes looked past the woman's florid self-satisfaction to the radiance of her kindly soul.

"Finally," Alison sighed as Sylvia sat down beside her. She put her glass on the floor and sighed again as Sylvia put her hands on her shoulders and kissed her cheek, unsure of her next move.

Alison's face and neck under her hands felt inert and distant. What she desired, she guessed, simply wasn't possible, so she dismissed it. The human body was warm, not cold; yet touching Alison, Sylvia thought of sunless stones and concrete laid over damp, cold ground. Fear clutched her and she sat back.

"It's sweet, your shyness," Alison said, taking Sylvia's hand and pressing it insistently to her breast.

That night, some time and much alcohol later, Sylvia awoke to find Alison with her cheek on one elbow, observing her with a vaguely menacing demeanor. As she sat up, Alison lit a new cigarette, remaining silent for a while, just watching Sylvia, who found herself a little nervy – sensing a portent of trouble. Alison, like a cat with its prey, gleamed. Then she made an outlandish confession. To get by, she announced, given that Han had left her high and dry, she'd taken to turning tricks on the street to pay the bills. Then she sat back snugly against the pillows, leaving the ball in her lover's court. Sylvia said nothing, wondering whether it could be some kind of joke.

"That night," Alison said, "I think you'll remember it – back on Judge Smith's block – on that dark stretch between the avenues, remember? There was a hooker."

"Yes, said Sylvia. She accosted Han. I thought she didn't look like a hooker … "

"Yes – her hair *was* blonde! And she was Han's *wife...*"

"It's not your fault," Sylvia blurted, not thinking. "It's the best response in the world. It's humiliating to him." Turning her head, she whispered, "and to me."

"Oh, really?" Alison hissed with hate. "You absolve me, then, of my obsessive lust?"

"I think it's the perfect response. It's symbolic."

"Symbolism sucks! But you don't! You moralize! Get out of here! Just get the hell out of here! On the double!"

Sylvia was afraid to turn her back on Alison's fury. She stretched over the table and picked up her bag. "I got paid today," she murmured. "The bank gave me brand new bills."

Mysterious and terrifying, Alison snapped up a proffered bill and put it under her glass. "Not bad pay for a let down," she smoldered. "Who are you anyway? You look in disguise, like an actress playing a part. Not a teacher. A banker? Are you an actress playing a banker?"

"You know I'm not an actress." Sylvia's elbows were giddy, even her knees. The giddy knees of an actress! "I'm a lawyer," she cried. "You bought me a drink. Last fall. We sat on the churchyard wall?"

"How much of my time did you waste then?"

Alison was hating an actress, not an ugly hick. Sylvia dipped into her purse for another bill and laughed as Alison plucked it up.

"I work on Wall Street. I'm way over-paid. "

"No one is overpaid." Alison reached for the whiskey bottle.

"Goodnight."

"Compared to you, I am. Look at the risks you take." She and Han were dishonorable! Their incredible selfishness had driven Alison to detach herself from her body so that its exploitation could make her independent of her faithless husband; so that she could pay her way. The process had gone so far that she even felt impersonal to touch.

"What risks?" Alison swallowed from the bottle. "Don't kid yourself. Look what they've got you wearing! Dull, schoolgirl gray. Knees together, smile in your voice, argue with a question mark... Listen, my dear, you can't be paid enough for that."

"I can wear bright colors if I want. This dress is good because it's neutral. It's good to de-emphasize the body in an office. It makes life easier."

"It makes you easier to ignore."

"I'm not ignored. I've already tried a case and I won it. It's very possible that I'll be a partner."

"A partner? Talk about my risk! You turn yourself into a little gray bunny, fixing it all for our corrupt corporations? To do that kind of job on the population? What else is Wall Street for?"

Sylvia felt attractive – as if Alison were singing her praises.

"It's called white collar crime," Alison growled as she rose and crashed against her. Walking on Sylvia's feet, boring her elbows into Sylvia's chest, she made for the kitchen. "White collar crime and she dresses like a nun. Curtsy!" Alison dipped down. "Yes, Sir. No, Sir. At least I can wear what I want."

Down the hall and into the kitchen, Alison, for all she'd drunk, was as steady as a tea room matron. "Check the pilot light on that crummy stove, one final twist to the faucets. Damn that son of mine for leaving on the light. She stopped, hearing a noise from the kitchen.

"What's that laugh? Doc!" Alison stepped up to the elusive doctor with a shout.

"Hey! You eccentric being! With your beautiful robes covered with dirt! Look who I have here, Doc – this young woman's along your line." Alison pulled Sylvia into the kitchen and held her hand.

"Just tonight – bold as brass and as unknown to me as you were when you crashed through that moldy tunnel door into the cellar – this woman commandeers me on the street."

Doc turned his head as he stood at the sink. In Alison's house, held within the circle of her arm, Sylvia's hostility to him died. Excited and flattered, she returned his friendly smile. As Alison put her arm around Doc's waist and smiled back at her, she felt she was deeply appealing to them both.

"I'm furious with this man for coming so late. No drink left. No fun!"

"I had an emergency drop across the way." Doc's hands were covered with pink foam. Foam clung to his white tunic and filled the holders of Alison's inherited silver candlestick which he was polishing in the sink. There were dirt stains on his shoulders and sleeves.

Alison's hands worked briskly as she rubbed away the dirt. Her heels lifted out of her shoes as she stretched and scolded him. "This beautiful material! Use the front door if you want to visit me, or, if you can't resist the tunnel, take off your tunic."

"I had my hands full tonight."

Quietly laughing, Doc turned back to his polishing. Alison spread her hands on his shaking shoulders and pressed her forehead, then her lips to his spine.

"Don't forget the lights when you leave, Doc," Alison called back, as she opened the front door for Sylvia to take her leave. "It's necessary to leave one light on for my gentleman callers!"

As Sylvia left the house she staggered, and her hip clipped the heavy doorknob. "Good," she muttered. "Staying so long, wasting her time, boring Alison to death."

Around the block, in the twin brownstone, Han had left on the kitchen light. Reaching into the cupboard, the whiskey bottle and the two-ounce jigger came into her hands like anesthesia. Sylvia drank from the jigger twice, then swallowed from the bottle as Alison had. Holding it close to her lips, her vigorous breath made lonely sounds as it passed over the opening. Her thick words were meaningless, but her thought was singular and clear. Alison was selfless and noble, but the demands of her desperate situation had warped her judgment. Her unflattering judgment of Wall Street was the temporary notion of a mortified, noble spirit.

Sylvia's emotion unfurled like a flag as she stumbled up the back stairs to Han's bedroom. She stood in front of the closet swinging apart the hangers in search of her brightest clothes. That longish purple skirt and the lavender blouse were a perfect pick for tomorrow. Harry Rodman could care less if by chance he noticed what she was wearing. He was always friendly and sometimes gay, but like many of the partners, he was way, way back in a cave of concentration which only his work had the power to penetrate.

An actress? Was she an actress? Alison's exciting voice had said those words. Insouciant to the amount of whiskey she'd drunk, Sylvia undressed, put away her clothes and went into the bathroom. She put down the toilet seat and sat up on the tank. Crossing her legs, she seriously regarded her face reflected in the mirror of the medicine chest an arm's length away.

The square mirror became Alison's admiring gaze. Apparently impervious to the sex Alison had instigated, so harsh and remote, Sylvia's nightly fantasy rekindled in her liquored brain. Always shy at first, her mouth and body were quiet beneath Alison's lips and hands. "I find you wildly attractive! Me, who's never looked twice at a woman before." Alison gently pushed her fingers through Sylvia's curls.

"Don't you dare fall asleep! Even if you do … I'll keep on kissing you …"

CHAPTER 17

"Han, do you think I look like an actress?" A few hours later, slumped at the kitchen table, Sylvia clutched her head in the early morning sun. "Harry Rodman says I do. Don't you think that's good?" She tapped Han's wrist as he put down the cereal box.

"You forgot the milk."

"Milk is rotten for hangovers. I'll make you some toast."

"What do you mean 'hangover'? Are you suggesting I got drunk with Harry Rodman?" Her upper lip twisted in her vivid sneer. "I've got some low-grade virus which is ruining my life. Stop smiling!"

"So that's why you wet the bed last night?"

"You peed on me. You haven't got the guts to admit you hate me, so you attack in the still of the night, coward! Oh, god! Will you ever stop smiling?" Han's affectionate amusement enraged her. "You should have been a head waiter. That's it! That's how you can support your father's drug habit when Doc cleans you out." Han held up the empty bottle, accusatory.

"I know nothing about your damn bottle. But I bet *Le Docteur* does – that thief."

"Outrageous!" He grasped her neck and gently shook her. "If you're sick you must go to the doctor."

"Western doctors treat the symptoms, not the cause. They don't know that first the heart craves pleasure." Swaying regally on the wooden chair, Sylvia folded her arms over her breasts and dropped her chin. "In some cultures, the body is the instrument

143

of the soul. The aches and pains, the tumors and stinging sinus cry out for the charm flower!"

Noticing her bright skirt as Sylvia stood, Han laughed with delight. "You're not going to work in that today?"

"You think it's too bright!" She grabbed at the material. "I'll be so late if I change."

"You look terrific! Give Rodman a break. "

"An excuse, you mean." Han was astonished at her suspicion, then wearily resigned. "Can't you ever believe that I'm rooting for you?" She was so absurdly hostile. "Now you look like an actress. You look as though you're choosing to distrust me."

"You might as well tell me to go to work naked. I hate you!"

"Sylvia!" His face and palms beseeched the ceiling. "You're hating yourself – the stupid associate, the would-be stupid partner. Working with Harry Rodman is making you miserable. "

Her teeth gleamed in her angry face. "It's you who's miserable! I'm doing fine! I've got more work than any other associate. I could spend twenty-six hours a day at the office and still I couldn't get it all done. All I have to do is remember about you and not blow it with gypsy clothes or any more of your advice." She stamped her feet. "Your unfailing sympathy! We both know I'm horrible! I should be put down like a sick dog!"

Han woke up later that night to find Sylvia at the foot of the bed, wearing the shirt he'd just thrown in the hamper buttoned up wrong. She held the whiskey bottle in both hands.

Her numb tongue and lips seemed to be receiving impulses from a brain as remote as its first disturbing memories. When she wasn't swallowing, Han heard sounds emerging from her as if from under ice, repeated and repeated.

"Not valid" he finally made out. *Not valid.*

"Go to the bathroom," he said sleepily in her ear, remembering that her urine was not made of ice.

In the early hours, still drunk, he awoke again to see that she'd shorn all her wonderful hair from her head. It reminded him now of the bushes in front of Harry Rodman's suburban home. Once luxuriant, her hair had been clipped to a dense, brusque curve, to geometric death, and a thought took hold of him.

"You're sleeping with that asshole, Harry Rodman!"

When she finally understood his roaring, her silvery, sophisticated laugh amazed him.

"Do you really think I'm sleeping with Harry Rodman? How wonderful."

"Damn you!" He fumed. "I found out you're corrupt after I fell in love with you. I hate you for that!"

"But I'm not." Her denial was almost negligible, "Imagine me being thought of as sleeping with the boss. Imagine me being thought sexy by men, by Harry Rodman."

"I'll never understand you!" Her smile terrified him. "Rodman's disgusting about women. Don't you know that?"

"I'm not having an affair with Harry Rodman!"

"But you want to."

She tossed up her chin at his contempt. "If I could get what you have, if I could steal it like Doc," she glowed with passion, "If I could, I'd drink your blood – if it was in your blood. If it was in an organ that I could swallow, I'd joyfully murder you! But I can't get it from you, and you can't teach me, and I really wish," he caught the falling chair as she stood up. "I really wish that I could quietly die."

"Because you think you're *not valid?*" He shouted.

Han's pulse was violent as he hung onto the bedpost. He wanted to weep in her lap and accept the peace of her lies, but instead he would dress, get his father's military sword from the study wall and drive across the river to the edge of New Jersey to Harry Rodman's house.

Yet, the practicalities of departure – opening a drawer for a shirt, finding his wallet and the keys to the car, were a nightmare of obstacle and delay. At last, dressed and reaching for the sword, he heard his father moan. He'd forgotten his father! Han slumped with relief at the sounds which nailed him fast to the house. It was five in the morning, a few minutes to go before his father's next dose of charm. Calling up to him, Han sat on the bottom steps of the third-floor stairs and reassuringly answered his every cry while he looked up Harry Rodman's phone number. Repeatedly writing the number down wrong, the pen was a dagger in his hand, and Harry Rodman's blood came blue.

"Hold on, Dad!" If the phone rang more than five times, he assumed he'd mis-dialled and tried again. Finally, he heard Rodman say, "hello."

"This is Hannibal Smith and I'm going to kill you if you spend one more night with Sylvia Stride."

The accusation obviously excited and flattered the partner. Rough spurts of laughter passed through the wires and into Han's surprised ears. He admitted that Sylvia Stride wasn't the 'dog' he'd first thought. Her looks had grown on him, but not nearly enough to make her his 'cup of tea.' He was like Han, even 'quickie' sex had to have class.

"I'm living with Sylvia Stride and I want to marry her. If you go back on your deal with her, if you try to transfer her back to Trusts and Estates, then I'm going to give Virginia Howe enough information to make her see an appeal as a very interesting prospect."

Although known for his hilarious sense of humor, Han heard the partner's alarm in his breathing.

CHAPTER 18

As Han waited for Sylvia to come down to the kitchen next morning, the radio forecast that the sunny morning was the beginning of a pleasant, late winter day. Then he killed the sound with a vicious twirl of his fingers, waiting for her routine morning rudeness to justify his fury.

Anger rushed up Han's spine as she came into the room. Clipped, sallow, vulnerable and subdued, Sylvia's gray dress fell from drooping shoulders in humble folds as she went to the table.

"Why are you lying about Harry Rodman?"

"I really regret you're going mad Han."

"Even you, Sylvia, can't argue with the facts." So clumsy and slow getting her own breakfast, he watched her small disasters with angry pleasure. "Your head looks exactly like the bushes in Harry Rodman's yard."

"This is madness."

"Have you told Harry Rodman that you think I'm insane?"

"Of course, I haven't." She was shocked at Han's calm distrust. "God knows I haven't.'"

"You must be sure also to tell him that crazy or not, I'm full of projects and that I carry them through to the end. That's very important for you."

Sylvia turned away. "If it comes up. If I see him."

"Tell him tonight."

"Tonight?" Sylvia groaned and tugged her hair. "I wish it was summer and we lived in the arctic. That the sun always shining and we had no nights. But, why should I be afraid of the night? What I don't want to do, I don't have to do. I'm not under a spell. Have you ever felt that you were suddenly just rushing over your will like water over a broken dam?"

Piling dishes in the sink, Han rinsed them, then bending again began to put them in the dishwasher. Sylvia's will like a broken dam? Wasn't that a virtual confession?

How Han hated her corruption, but considering her suffering every morning, how could he hate her? Sleeping with the boss was so normal, she'd wistfully suggested. But Rodman's sleazy puritanism was turning her body to wood. A human shadow descended the front steps to the sidewalk; Sylvia was going to work. *If I could, I'd drink your blood ...* She did love him.

But she *was* having an affair with Harry Rodman! It was more obvious with every step she took from the house. That pushy, seedy, little man – Han wiped his brow with a dish towel – how could she? Because she was ambitious! That ferrety jack in her box was aroused by her ambition, not her heart.

Lost in thought for some time, Han felt the height of the clouds and the swift darts and twirls of the wind, darts of shadow too. Then he suddenly jumped a foot at the ringing phone.

"Sylvia? I just saw you go out the door. Is it really ten?" Han blocked his eyes to see the clock against the sun. "I didn't know it was so late. I was thinking about you."

Han's dawn phone call had astonished Harry Rodman, Sylvia told him. He couldn't understand where Han was coming from and really, neither could Sylvia. Pleased and thankful, her voice put him on the edge of tears.

"You come home so late now. Every night."

She laughed. "You know that downtown there was no such word as 'late'."

"You're so miserable in the morning – the way you hate your body."

"That was just my fatigue speaking, "she said. "You shouldn't pay any attention."

"Why did you cut your hair?"

"Holy hell, that *was* a mistake, wasn't it?" She agreed. "Yet hair has a reputation for growing back and so why not mine? Really Han, you must believe me! Harry Rodman compared to you? Impossible! Gross – very bad!"

"I don't understand you," he croaked.

"But hey – thanks for implicating me in such a *normal* scenario – I feel much better now!"

Exalted, Han stepped out onto the back steps. The pool in the center of the garden was glittering in the strong sun. When he closed his eyes to better hear her tender, frank voice – no lie could hide in that tone – gold dazzled the inside of his eyelids.

Yet, who knows how much later, the next time he opened his eyes, the pool had turned black under clouds. Bitch!

CHAPTER 19

"Why can't I read today?" Han been botching lines since he'd begun. Such afternoons had become his routine, caring for his father, pandering to his every demand, and often just sitting at the side of the judge's bed, reading. Furious at the sound of his own hesitant voice, Han wanted his father's sarcasm.

"I'm such a fool!"

His father turned his weary eyes from the sunlight on the wall and pitied him.

"You don't look well. The weather's so changeable now. Are you coming down with a cold?"

"My wife is leaving me."

"Darling! I can't count the times your mother took herself off. For instance, where is she now? But she'll be back. So will Alison."

The room seemed huge around his father's neat, frail form.

"But, she's in love, dad. She loves another man!"

"Women flail about – need attention. Alison married the best and she's stuck with the best. You'll see. But you're haggard. You've got to get out into the sun and air. I'm perfectly comfortable for at least two hours after lunch, get over to the river promenade or do the reservoir – put some roses in your cheeks.   I just need my medication".

"I'm giving you a bit extra today, dad." Han slipped in a second needle. "I'm going to go out for a long run during your nap. This will keep you comfortable in case I'm held up."

"Held up, dear boy? Not you. Nothing's going to hold you up."

As Han walked along in the bright, breezy afternoon, a chipper construction worker was talking to his friend as he walked by.

"Tomorrow, I'm taking my ass downtown."

The idea that one could be the master of one's ass wrapped Han briefly in the same relief as his father's mellow platitudes. Han had come to understand Sylvia's look of grave absorption when she listened to his Pleasantville stories. Immersion in ordinary, everyday life was intensely comforting. In a similar way, in his father's mind, being Alison's husband was to step into a benign fairyland. Then to escape on his run every afternoon - to step out to the brash street, anonymous and desolate, Han understood that, too. The loneliness of the windy street, with his identity now tucked in his father's sleeping brain.

Recently, the deepest sleep his father enjoyed occurred in the middle of the afternoon, allowing Han to run his ass in the park, where he was a nasty coach: "Get in gear! Move it, god damn it!"

The day before, however, near the street where he lived, a shocking event had stopped his loutish game. Out of the blue, Han had run into his own sons – in uptown Manhattan. Now, he hurried through the cold, bright streets looking for them again.

During his run, Peter had galloped past him, looking graceful yet determined. A street kid was chasing him. Han turned as they sped by and saw another boy zip off a bench and stick his foot between Peter's ankles. When the boy straddled him and tugged him up, Peter saw a policeman and shouted out: "Officer! Officer!"

Letting Peter go, the kid bellowed: "He stole smoke! He stole smoke, officer!" The policeman stared phlegmatically.

"If you're selling it, then tough shit." Peter trotted off at the policeman's side as the street kids bounded away in the opposite direction, hooting and slapping each other's palms. Han had hardly caught up to where the scene had taken place when his other son ran casually up to him as if the whole previous chaotic month had not occurred.

"Dad! Peter stole pot from those kids."

Han held out his arms, then slowly lowered them. Freddy's face, almost hidden by his thick, untrimmed bangs, looked calm. Han moved to a bench. He patted the slats as he sat down, but Freddy stayed put. He spread his legs, folded his arms and looked calmly through his blond hair.

"Where have you been, dad?"

"I've missed you, darling! I've missed you so much!" All previous evening, tending to his father, Freddy had dominated Han's thoughts and feelings. Without having gained a pound, the boy seemed to have grown up; grown solid.

Freddy's mouth twisted to a vicious sneer. "Darling? You don't say that. Only Mother does."

Han looked down. "Unexpectedly, I found myself on vacation."

"Mother said you couldn't come to Europe because you had an important case."

"I've been living with someone."

"Why?"

"I fell in love."

The fling of his hair from his brow revealed Freddy's violent confusion. "No! You're taking care of grandpa and you're having an affair with his nurse. We live in the other brownstone now — until the house upstate is fixed. We watch you from our window."

Freddy turned to walk away.

"You're disgusting!"

Han ran after him and gripped his shoulder at the curb, "That's my friend. She's not a nurse, she's a lawyer."

"I don't care what she does." Freddy suddenly drove his fist into Han's side and broke away from him, crossing the street. "Don't walk near me!" Freddy called Han an asshole at every step as they walked up the block. "Why don't you love mother anymore?"

"I don't know."

"Asshole! She doesn't love you either!" Freddy darted off. Han followed him around the corner and there he was, sitting on the broad church steps, his hair swept back from his face.

"Mother's got a new boyfriend and he's huge. He could beat the shit out of you!"

"So could you." Han respectfully felt his side. "You've gotten so strong!"

"I go to public school. Peter couldn't take it."

That Alison should lead a squatter's existence in the house and commandeer a new lover was unsuspected but not a surprise. Peter's apparent physical passivity made Han's heart ache, but did not surprise him either. It didn't even bother him too much that his son now considered him promiscuous and disloyal. Yet Freddy's mistaking Sylvia's social position and proclaiming, "I don't care what she does" alarmed the hell out of him. Good God, was he really such a snob?

Han hurried after Freddy, in the direction of the neighborhood's public school, dodging round thick clusters of black children. Could they all really be so vital and good looking? The smell of marijuana had been faint, but now, in a burst, it was strong. Turning his head, Han looked into a rudely impersonal face.

"I got good stuff, policeman."

"I'm not a policeman. I'm looking for my son."

"Buy from me, policeman. I've got the best."

"I'm really not interested. I assure you." Han dismissed the boy with a frigid smile. "I'm neither a policeman nor a spy. I'm looking for my son."

Staring again through the fence his spine tingled with alarm. As he turned and crossed the street to look for Freddy, Han inwardly quailed at the wave of intelligent menace that emanated from the dark faces. All the way to the avenue, Han was intensely aware of his back. He turned the corner and stood shivering against a wall.

"Bastards," he muttered.

Suddenly, he spotted Freddy, who was walking along the street close to the curb, a slice of pizza folded in his hand. A muscular black boy put his hand on his shoulder and pointed to the slice.

"No!" Freddy – grinned. "I'm hungry! Buy your own." The boy loomed over Freddy and smiling, stepped on his sneaker.

"Hey!" Han stepped forward. His fist hung in the air as Freddy turned his back.

"I see your point," Freddy cheerfully handed over the pizza. "You're big."

The boy laughed as he bit and handed back the diminished slice. Then he backed off and joined another boy as huge as himself and the two of them strode off.

His father's next dose of charm was not due for another half hour, so he decided to keep following Freddy. These kids were everywhere. Han stopped by a delivery truck and watched the street kids' reflection in its windshield. His memory added strength and size to the kids moving in the glass. Every face wore a revolutionary mask to Han's mind – hatred perfectly controlled. Freddy was in danger!

He remembered the previous night, as, anguished, Han had wanted to go after the boys, but his father's increasing pain had propelled him home to the brownstone. Propped on pillows, the Judge's thick hair and eyebrows seemed like the froth of his fierce anger. His commanding hand waved Han from his view.

"God damn it, Han! Don't just gape down at me! Turn the damned television on!"

On the screen, the news was about how the city was closing down a hospital in Harlem to save money. The screen was jammed with furious, protesting faces.

"Here we go!"

Han sagged with fear. Tomorrow morning, he would intercept Freddy on his way to school. "It's starting, dad, just as you predicted. The riots."

"Nothing's starting, for Christ's sake, which you'd know if you were watching – but you don't watch, you dream."

"But dad. You said the cities were a powder keg."

"God damn it, where's your brain, boy? The cities are flooded with drugs – marijuana, cocaine … The strongest heroin in years is on every inner city street corner. Drugs and revolution don't mix. These people sit in front of the TV sniffing, injecting, inhaling." His gray tongue darted from his mouth.

"Dreams! That's all that happens. A sentimental, dreamy people, foolish, emotional, just like you. God damn it, Han! You've made yourself into a servant, a nurse, a houseboy, so you can dream your life away. A timid, credulous, ignorant nursemaid, that's what you've become."

Hoping that the previous day's impression of racial menace would prove to be subjective and trying to put the scene with his father out of his mind, Han set off on the way to the public school with a brave whistle. Perhaps, when he reached the school, his father's unfocused youth were what he'd see. But their numbers and size were just as he remembered, and again Han met that unnerving look, that impressive blend of hatred and control.

Intending to circle the playground on the inside, Han walked quickly through the gate and before long, among the endless clusters of casual players, the generous color and zingy movement, he saw Freddy – putting his best into a game of basketball! His new solid look was impressive even in the midst of such height. Deftly, he cut to the basket. Hitting the rim, the ball shot to the side. Freddy raced for it. Large and smiling, the boys waited. He was tripped as he dribbled and lunged wildly. He jumped against a boy and delivered the ball into a pair of quick hands. He came down hard on his duff, laughed and tossed back his hair.

Han sprang forward, his hand pointing. "That's unfair! Give him a chance."

"Shit, man. The judge is here!" Said one voice, prompting laughter from the other boys.

Gay, bold faces fixed on Han. "Hey, boy! Give the judge's son the ball." A broad, mocking path was cleared to the basket and with exaggerated bows and looks of solicitude, the ball was courteously placed in Freddy's hands.

"Fuck it!" Freddy slammed it down and walked off, furious.

Han kept well behind this anger as they walked away from the hoots and laughter. Passing the school, they'd gone a mile along the avenue before Han dared to walk beside his son.

"They were roughing you up!"

"You're a fool!" Although blushing and breathless, Freddy's tone was calm.

"These are dangerous times," Han pleaded. "It's not safe to be alone in a mob!"

"You mean the playground?" Freddy sneered. "You're a fool – an idiot, like Peter."

"Don't you feel the hostility? It's terrifying."

The blood stayed in Freddy's face, but his voice was husky and even. "Only with you. You look so snotty – frowning at everybody." He twisted his features into a mirror grimace. "I'd mug you if I was from around here. I'd kill you!"

Feeling his brows, Han was astonished. He hadn't known he'd been frowning. More disturbing was the fact that Freddy had just showed him the Judge's face, with its frigid condemnation. Was it possible that Freddy could have seen that in Han's features? The idea repelled Han.

"Oh, come on! I'm not like that!" He pleaded, dropping onto a bench. "I'm just worried about you!"

His face still crimson, Freddy started walking backwards along the river walk, shooting his arm out to point at Han. 'You left – now stay away! Nobody wants you back. Not mother, not Peter, not me! Stay away!"

In in a panic, out of breath, Han tried to follow his son – but lost him on the way home. Before he went upstairs to deliver the judge's dose of charm, Han stood in his own back yard, in the mournful evening light, looking up at the brownstone on the other side of the pool. It was like a black wall, that house. Perfectly black. How did Alison manage that? Layers of curtains? Had she painted the glass?

In this bizarre proximity, sealed and censored, Han felt his separation from his family for the first time. The muffled wall was a boundary of the known. Before, the Pleasantville pictures that Han recalled in his mind, to be dutifully banished, included him, and were comfortable and familiar. But that black wall! Freddy's hard, blank eyes. What went on behind both was new and ominous.

He found himself shouting.

"Freddy!" He shouted.

"Freddy!" Came the echo off the dark, solid wall of the opposite house. For a long time, nothing. Then, materializing at the kitchen steps, there was his son.

"Hey, dad."

Han turned around, lunged towards the house and sank down.

"You're here!"

"I'm sorry I said what I said. I'm really sorry."

"I'm sorry about sending you to dig for gold. Your mother and I thought it was such a joke. I'm exactly who I never wanted to be! I'm my father. How in hell did I get to be my father?"

A frightening silence flowed from Freddy.

"You never even called. I hate you!" He stooped down on the gravel path and picked up a rock, firing it at Han, who hopped and clutched at his knee. "I hope I broke it!" He yelled.

"Good shot!" Han whistled in pain. Christ, what an arm.

"How about some supper, Freddy? Come on! You used to love French toast. I'll fix you some in a second. Come on!"

Flaring with pleasure despite himself, Freddy stepped towards him, then, bewildered, guilty, he planted his feet and folded his arms across his chest. "Stuff it up your ass! Up your ass!" He howled.

It was only after the violent slam of the back door that Han could begin to run out of rage, could say to himself that the child's anger was an aspect of his pride, and turn back to his own house. Of course, Freddy could not forgive him immediately, even if he wanted to, and the more Han complied with his dictatorial rudeness, the sooner it would end. Han was the runaway asshole, Mr. Vacation Man and the Dumbest Daddy Dude around.

As he closed the kitchen door behind him, Han knew he wouldn't be going to the school yard again. But Freddy, in a storm of guilty anger, would sooner or later be coming to him. Han opened the refrigerator and peered into the cupboards in front of the stove. The barrenness of supply would discourage a second trip, if indeed, Freddy made it once. But he'd come. Not tomorrow, perhaps, not even this week – but soon.

CHAPTER 20

The next morning Han found the supermarket the most congenial place in the world.

As he idled down the aisles of cereals, he rejoiced in the brazen blare of the boxes. In Pleasantville the boys had each breakfasted behind his own tall box. Wasn't it Freddy who liked the brand with the nature series on the back? Honey Comb, Captain Crunch, Han examined their names as he turned the cartons over. Here it was. Frosted Flakes. All over the city, in the morning, how many of these radiant boxes blocked school nerves, even dread while the cereal was chewed and sucked, and the sweet milk swallowed?

Hot dogs, chicken legs, Hamburger, steak, French Fries, ice cream, cookies and soda. Han would make sure that when the boys looked out at the Judge's house it would always blaze with light, the kitchen a paradise. Han spent an age before the case of frozen food.

The next evening, sooner, rather than later, Freddy popped across the yard for dinner. With dirty hair and a tough face, he put his sneakers up on the table, framing the best china in the house. Han thought himself too numb for resentment until he heard Freddy's:

"I can't eat this shit," and saw the pizza he had prepared drop to the floor. Then he was across the kitchen in a bound. Freddy snatched up a steak knife.

"Come on, asshole! I'll rip you even if I don't take you. Oh, come on!"

"How'd you get like this? You used to be a nice kid." Hands up in surrender, smiling, Han regretted his stupidity.

"I used to be like Peter and you." Throwing the knife down beside his plate, Freddy slammed the back door.

The following day, when Freddy showed up, Han was ready for him, having roasted a whole chicken with all the trimmings. Even his earnest culinary efforts, however, evaded the boy's approval. There was a horrid smack on the linoleum floor as Freddy tossed a chicken bone, missing the garbage pail by a few inches. Han went to pick it up.

"Oh, god! Look at the pussy! He's drying his hands before he picks up the bone."

As Han knelt, a second bone landed on his shoulder. The explosion from the table, the squeal and bray of that adolescent laughter, converted Han's fury to amusement. He dropped the remains of his beautifully cooked chicken in the garbage and went back to the dishes. The silence was awful.

"So … what did you learn about in school today, anyway?" Han asked, expecting more insults.

"Genes, you jerk!"

But then Freddy suddenly launched into a long monologue about Peter. Feet on the table, smoking, Freddy's face was hidden behind his sneakers. With a nervous rasp of his throat, he ventured, "In biology class I finally found out why Peter's such a pussy. Because you are!"

"Really?"

"Really." Freddy squealed a vile imitation, then softened as he had the night before. "Why doesn't Peter see that mother's different now? He's so stupid! Really stupid!" His darting eyes fixed on Han. "We're not allowed to come over here. Even though Peter knows I've been five times and nothing's happened, he thinks mother will know if he disobeys her. He forgot to wash the kitchen floor. You should have seen him."

Han saw Peter exactly in Freddy's portrayal of his brother's dismay. "Oh, Jesus! She'll have my ass! The mop's gone! Where's the mop? Where is it? I'm dead." Laughing quietly, Freddy sank back on his chair. "But mother doesn't check on us for anything anymore. Not since we moved in from the country. Oh, once in a while, but hardly ever. Still, Peter acts as though she's got X-ray eyes and intercom ears. The jerk believes she has magic powers. Everyone does over there. Like that friend of hers who comes over every night." Freddy's face assumed a sweetly frazzled expression that Han found familiar.

"She walks around like there's a tiny man on her shoulder who keeps hitting her on the head with a hammer. Mother's got her working like a slave, got her tutoring Peter and cleaning the house. Last night mother wanted the oven cleaned. Guess what?" Freddy's eyes glowed with sad astonishment, "Sylvia cleaned it in her dress. I kept telling her to stop, that I'd do it, but she was on automatic pilot. Pathetic!"

The gray dress Han had picked off the closet floor this morning was so badly stained that the dry cleaner wouldn't guarantee the job.

"What did you call her? The friend?"

"Sylvia." Freddy sighed. "She comes every night. Usually, mother goes out and leaves her working, but last night, mother had her drinks in the kitchen and *watched* her. 'Sparingly, darling, that's expensive stuff. Those paper towels aren't free, you know.' I asked mother later if she was paying her and she said, 'What's that public school doing to you? One doesn't pay one's friends,' *One*. One doesn't pay one's friends!"

Han smiled at the perfect reproduction of Alison's grandeur.

"Both of them are like, hypnotized? Why?"

Han was too startled by his sensation of relief to respond. So Sylvia was not downtown every night – just next door.

"Peter thinks you're an honorable man because that's what mother tells him to think. That is so pathetic!" As Freddy swung open the kitchen door, his jaunty negligence turned Han into a fussy servant rushing to block the cold night air. "Swanson's fried chicken is much better than yours. But I don't care."

"I love you," Han laughed. "You're a wonderful boy."

"Up your ass," came the laconic reply.

Han hurried up to his father, as eager as he for the eight o'clock injection and the activation of the large TV screen. Sitting just behind the walnut bed, the friendly borders of the busy mirror would encourage him to think. Alison in place of Harry Rodman, no trouble there, no trouble at all – but his relief! That was extraordinary. As he watched the string of evening programs that his father liked Han rocked and shivered and smiled in the appreciation of what he'd suppressed since marrying Alison – that hatred turned outward was an ecstasy of relief – oh, god, he hated her!

He hated her and it wasn't his fault. He was no more to blame than Sylvia for Alison's fierce discontent. Stepping out of a thousand fairy tales, Alison was the wicked witch. She was!

CHAPTER 21

Over the previous couple of weeks, Sylvia had learned the different silences of Alison's house and this one – depression that made her yawn – meant that she and Freddy were the only occupants. They were finishing up the laundry.

"You're the most modern person I've ever met." The boy said, taking up one end of the basket, startling Sylvia with the opacity of his gaze.

"I'll take that as a compliment," she answered, lifting the other side of the basket, doubtful that it was meant as any such thing.

"No," he said, tossing his hair, "In fact, you're not. You're a machine. I've only known you for two weeks and I can predict everything you say and do – including your saying, *I'll take that as a compliment* and telling me about doing the laundry with your mother when you were a kid. You say it exactly the same way too, as if you've been programmed."

Sylvia was so tired she couldn't contradict Freddy's foolishness. Instead, she stood in the door a moment, straining for a sound in case Alison come back into the house while they'd been working. Then, she lifted her raincoat off the hook, took up her briefcase and said: "It was frantic at the office, today. I obviously got the time wrong. Will you please tell your mother I waited as long as I could, that I'm sorry I missed her?"

"Hold it!" Freddy zipped out of the kitchen. "Count to sixty," he yelled from the stairs. "I'll be back in a minute."

The sounds of his voice and shoes were forlorn explorers in the empty house. Sylvia stared at the place where the old stove had been until Freddy jumped back into view, his tape recorder slung across his shoulders.

"I got proof," he flicked a dial. "That's you two nights ago. Didn't I tell you? Listen – word for word what you told me to tell mother just now…" Her recorded voice sounded out in the dark hall.

Sylvia was terrified. "Do you tape me often?"

He sneered. "I never record anything but music. You just happened to walk in at the right time."

"Why shouldn't a normal message be standardized?"

"Word for word? That's what you always say when mother's not here." Freddy sped round the kitchen like a high-speed robot. "Machine clean house like hell!"

"Like hell," she lightly chided. "Sure, I help your mother out. At home," she pointed west, "that's called doing your chores."

"You washed a ton of laundry tonight. The other day you ruined your dress cleaning the oven."

Sylvia laughed at his skepticism. "I've been doing housework since I was five years old. It was a large family and my mother needed help." Suddenly, she was furious. "Anyway! I wanted to help my mother. I loved to help her!"

"That's sick."

"What?" Sylvia dropped her briefcase and made fists in angry bewilderment. "Your mother's so worried these days. She's over-worked, so tired. I feel sorry for her."

Smiling, Freddy fitted his hands over her tight fingers.

"You're nice, Sylvia, but, boy, are you dumb."

Outside on the dark street, her anger at Freddy welled up. A little prince with his prerogatives of food and shelter! It was dreadful, the lack of respect, courtesy and obedience that Peter showed his mother when in actuality, wasn't he like an infant or an ill-trained pet in his total dependence? Watching television with a packed stomach while Alison, panicked by the latest bill, ran to the streets to pick up men! How dare he?

On the avenue, Sylvia anxiously studied the hundred dark forms for a cherished detail of her ill-used friend. She refused any assistance offered by Sylvia, suffered the danger and vileness of picking up men and going to their apartments, all so that her sons could lounge in warmth and plenty. At *least* Peter studied.

"If I repeat myself it's because I'm so tired. I've got a virus and I can't, can't, can't get rid of it…" she said urgently to herself. "Oh, stop! Why not fall into the street, fool! Plunge under a truck..." Freddy's little number with the tape recorder, what did that prove? In a normal person, an exact repetition of expression was unusual, but possible, and the little charmer had caught it. So what?

It seemed an age ago now, but it was only two weeks since, on this same walk back from Alison's, that she'd first felt this misery – its aches and sweats and nausea no more or less intense, perfectly bearable, but frightening in its constancy. Yet she wouldn't lightly give up its anesthetic effect. In this low state, her gleaning of the insurance files, compared to her earlier ordeal with Han, was practically painless. Endurance substituted for alacrity and her eleven- and twelve-hour days were stacking up points in her favor.

The streetlights were off, and the birds were still quiet when Han awoke before dawn to hear Sylvia singing.

"What cheer, Netop!"

"You're drunk'" He sat up in bed.

"That was the chief's gracious greeting when Roger Williams met the Rhode Island Indians. A decent netop. Nice man." Sylvia's desolate face in the dim light of the window belied her sprightly air. "The Roger Williams Insurance Company is a new client in the office. I've just been assigned."

"And have you heard the news?" Flourishing the whiskey

bottle, Sylvia forced a big smile. "It's here. The weekend! Get drunk, dance, enjoy!"

She drank hard from the bottle and smacked it into his hands. She reached for the transistor on the bedside table and perched it on her shoulder like a parrot.

"Dance? Why not? Just dial up a tune." Somber, syrupy chords poured from her shoulder. "Free form, Han, the poses of my day: subway, office - what cheer for the heroic clerk? Look!"

Han waited for her to dance. But she didn't.

"But, I don't seem to move! Alright, then. Off the interpretive. I'm the literal, no nonsense type. Bottle, please!"

Han, impatient with her banter, became a snappish schoolmaster. As though it was a grammar mistake, he sat up in bed and began to address and correct what he had so long feared to utter – Sylvia's mistaken belief that she was in love with Alison.

"I never said that," she protested.

"You don't remember telling me you were in love with Alison? Really? You seemed conscious last night – you said you were in love with Alison..."

By the time she woke up again to go to work, Sylvia saw Han's accusation on the ceiling and knew that he was right. She resolved that these nights of mortifying disappointment were finished. She would call Alison from the office this morning to say that if they couldn't have dinner together, that night was off.

Full of dread, at eleven o'clock Sylvia reached for the phone. The fear of rejection slowed her heart. Foolish to court such pain. Alison would never have dinner with her.

After several rings, when Alison picked up the phone on the other end, it seemed barely credible... But she would? Oh, really, would she? Victory perched on the window ledge.

"I was praying that you would call," Alison crooned. "I've paid a fortune for steak and enough worthy wine to ensure a good talk!"

Victory! In front of the solid blue square of window glass in her tiny office, Sylvia jumped high. She talked to the gray sky beyond the large office window. Yet, never had her mind been so slow, so hard to drive. Sylvia watched her hands pull open the file, separate papers, carry a bunch to her desk, where her finger swept down the margins, apparently performing for its own sake, since her eyes sure weren't following, let alone her brain. 'Any fool can suffer through two hours,' she told herself. 'Come on! Come on! Her eyes and jaws ached in a clench of concentration and again Sylvia was startled that beneath her moving hand, the document was meaningless.

"Will power," Sylvia clamped her hands to her temples. "Will and endurance, that's all you've ever needed. You've been sicker than this." What an astonishing morning! She put her hand on her brow, her eyes closing from the comfort. She couldn't stop thinking about Han's saying, in his comradely tone: "It's not *love* with Alison, you know. It's something else."

"Not now, dummy: pull down the blinds until it's time to go to lunch."

When lunchtime finally came, Han's imagined voice rang in her ears as she crossed the lane to Doc's place and pulled open the pale blue door. Was she now patronizing the thieving Doctor? How amazing! Sylvia paused on the doorstep, the edge of the door handle hurting her palm. But it wasn't the owner, it was the simple, well cooked food that drew her here. For all she knew, Doc was uptown at Alison's, knee deep in ancient plaster or the polish that he so assiduously applied to the stolen antiques from Han's house across the way.

Slipping into the bar, Sylvia put off her confusion as she smiled at the restaurateur. Enemies at the prince's mansion, their menial services offered to the witch had made them humorous friends. As Doc plucked the 'reserved' sign off the dark corner table and hung up her raincoat they talked about Freddy.

"Freddy doesn't understand what's been done to his mother. He's too young. If Freddy knew where the money was coming from – if he ever does understand this thing, he'll see the point to our efforts. He'll be grateful." Had she always sounded so tepidly inauthentic? Was it just a convenient assumption that her drudgery and his theft were inspired by idealism?

"No!"

Startled at her fierce exclamation, the cook, on his way to her table with her order, shyly retreated towards the kitchen. She beckoned him back. "No, not you - I was daydreaming!" She took the plate from his hand, picked up the burger and took a bite, savoring the delicious meat and cheese, the juices spurting into her mouth. The cook brightened as he watched her. Sylvia waved at the kitchen when he got back and turned her mind inward with new resolution.

No. She and Doc had often laughed at the justice of his stealing for Alison, certainly, she'd not made up their idealistic complicity. She could not have told Han she was in love with Alison, because that was not the case. It was feminist morality that drew her passion and her time – her outrage at the incredible injustice of her friend's position!

The fading of her mental turmoil made her virus easy to bear. Drinking coffee, relishing the mild aches as the measure of her relief, Sylvia felt a long distance from the scene with Han at breakfast this morning.

She waved goodbye to the Japanese cook as she went out the door and noticed that it pleased and excited her to walk into the crowd of men on the packed sidewalk. She liked the glances, the voices and the chance touch of an arm or shoulder. Positively, she liked what had numbed her before. A few more months with Han – the attractive young man and woman beginning their day with breakfast in the kitchen – and the normalcy he had imparted to her surface would seep inward to her core.

Yet, once she entered again into the powerful confines of the law firm, Han's shock that morning swept back into her mind and the keen of the rising elevator became the sound of fear. Even when her office door hid her from the crowd of lawyers outside, her sensation of exposure was excruciating.

"You don't remember telling me you were in love with Alison? Really? You seemed conscious last night —"

Sylvia sat staring out of her office window. Apparently, she'd told him that, but she didn't remember! Terrified, Sylvia rocked as a chill breeze came in the window. When all she recalled was a nightcap or two at the end of a long, righteous day, was she also, actually, every night, drinking her mind dead? The contemptible creature that remained, that said to Han that it loved Alison, was that thing — a lesbian?

Sylvia forced her back straight and looked down at her lap. Her hands settled separately, one on each knee. Their shape and color had always pleased her and as a child, when depressed, they'd become the hands of another person, someone noble and aloof, whose rare touch distinguished only her. The window rattled in the wind, which howled shrill and sharp like the wind of her home in the west. She'd been a fat child and the feeling of her large, soft stomach was again on her arms. "Mother's lump " was what her brothers had called her. The baby of the family, the only girl, stapled to her mother. She worried when her brothers began to laugh at her. "Sylvia doesn't know what to wear to school. She says mother hasn't told her."

When she started falling down, their advice was simplicity itself. "Forbid her, mother." When her mother had cut her hair, shined her shoes and packed the trunk that was bound for college, Sylvia had slumped on the bed, the outfit picked out for the journey crushed beneath her legs. She didn't want to leave home, she'd wept, she wasn't ready.

Dark and fierce, her mother pushed on the trunk while she

shouted. She'd gotten Sylvia ready! Her brain was too good for this provincial place with its dinky institutions. That brain was leaving here, and it wasn't coming back again without prizes and honors to adorn her mother's walls.

A package of her mother's ambition, Sylvia accompanied her luggage to college and then to the east coast, legs and arms finally sprouting, she'd scarcely been home since they'd grown.

Han liked her body, said her legs were elegant and admired the shape and strength of her arms. Legs to take her places, arms to grasp and keep. Could she ever reach for the things her mother had disdained in her grueling race: pleasure, love and gaiety? It hadn't been long since she'd sat with Han at Doc's place, a sliver of time since that first evening, when Han said that her anger became her, that he'd just seen her as beautiful.

When she was a child, she'd thought her mother was beautiful and once she'd told her so. Well, she must fancy herself, her mother had mocked, for Sylvia looked just like her – un-tender. Her mother toiled for her family. Cooking, cleaning, coaching, checking, there was always sweat on her brow.

But now, in turn – Sylvia toiled for Alison! Last night she'd done the boys' laundry and changed their beds while Alison watched television and drank. She was gratified by Alison's gruff announcement that the promised dinner was way beyond her strength this evening. Whistling softly, she'd made Alison a sandwich and delighted in her hungry bites. She'd even smiled, on leaving the house, at Alison's farewell:

"Sometime I'll teach you how to make a decent sandwich."

But outside, on the street, Sylvia's smile had faded. They were all just swept, Alison had once said. To hope, to torture, to bliss.

Night after night, remote as the stars, the yellow windows of Han's house showed the same mysterious pattern to her frightened gaze. Drinking whiskey in the kitchen, the ceiling vibrated in service to Han's mysterious faith as he sought the system of sound waves to pulse along his father's nerves that would annul the advancing waves of pain. On the sea of her brain, the crests of the liquor waves tumbled into troughs of pain, tumbled, tumbled, until consciousness was golden, smooth and still.

Still transfixed at her office window, Sylvia leaned forward and pressed her cheek against the cold glass. South, where Han always looked, clouds rested on the horizon. Color gave them weight and Sylvia saw her home mountains, saw the ponderous curiosity of Pleasantville.

Desperately, she picked up the phone and called Han.

"I never told you I loved Alison! I couldn't have, because I don't. I know what you're trying to do. Harry Rodman snubbed me twice today, so I know what you're trying to do."

Seeking the comfort of his voice, she barely understood what Han was saying in response, just ploughed on.

"First, Rodman hears that he's sleeping with me and next that I'm in love with your wife and you're *laughing*." Passionately focused on the affectionate tone of his response, she couldn't understand Han's explanation of Harry Rodman's coldness. Soon, she didn't care. Her terror was passing, that tone made all the difference. Han loved and respected her – she could hear it in his voice. But she persisted all the same.

"You couldn't stand it if they made me a partner. You'll sink me. I know it." The patient litany of Han's denial was cheerful as bells. She wouldn't go to Alison's that night, she resolved calmly. Dinner or not.

"I won't be working tonight," she told Han. "I'll have dinner with you for a change."

"I won't go to Alison," she told herself, voice raised aloud. At her desk, her chin propped on her fist, Sylvia felt no emotion. No anxiety, no guilt, no yearning. "I've made the connection, that's why." Sylvia prized the money and time she saved by being as clever as a psychiatrist.

"Alison's not noble. It's her voice. Her voice is like mother's. I've escaped her already. It's because I'm free of mother that Alison's got herself such a sucker. It's guilt, that's all, and it's over. I'm all paid up – and I love a man."

172

CHAPTER 22

"Ooooooh ... "

Han smiled back at Sylvia over his shoulder as they climbed the stairs. "Dad makes that sound when he wakes up. After his shot, he purrs. Come on. He's been asking about you."

A light wind in a hollow place, the sound continued as she followed Han.

"I'm coming, dad. You're right on schedule and so am I. Everything's the same except that Sylvia's not working tonight. She's here, dad, and impatient to see you."

A rosy ceiling light dimly lit the room. Sylvia stayed back as Han stepped inside a circle of speakers and leaned over the high four poster bed. When he drew down the blankets, a sharp smell, a smell of decaying, wet leaves, frightened her. Her gaze fastened on the neatly packed shelves of a huge open wardrobe. There were piles of bed linen, diapers folded in triangles, baby oil, baby powder, hypodermic needles on a tray and a shelf of glass jars.

"Ooooooh."

"Now, you know I can't give you the ten o'clock dose until I clean you up a bit. You'll insist on walking to the bathroom and the doctor's forbidden you to get out of bed. I know you think old Adams is a fool, but we're paying him for his advice and so we'll take it."

Sylvia marveled at Hans' competence and the humorous respect of his voice and manner. "Even I know that no one moves a muscle with hepatitis. That's right. You're not allowed out of bed until Adams sees you again. Just grin and bear it."

Han ran his fingers along the inside of the judge's arm, back and forth, his eyes grimly following. He took the hypodermic needle from the table and with a triumphant nod, pushed the needle into a vein. "Hooray for 10 p.m. Hooray for the double dose!"

Han's jacket pulled tight across his back as he folded his arms and watched his father. Frightened by his severity, Sylvia pressed against the door frame with all her might. Slowly she relaxed as Han did. Propping three pillows against the headboard, he quickly swept the judge up against them.

"Partners coming at me!"

"Partners?" Han leaned closer to the frail, gray head.

"Poking and picking!"

Han looked where his father pointed. "Look, dad, I haven't ruined my career so that you can continue yours. We've got a lot of reading left to do."

"In my dreams."

"Ah, dreams," Han threw off with mild disinterest. "Is the dose okay? Do you need more?"

"I feel wonderful."

"Sylvia Stride has come to see you, dad."

"Who is Sylvia?" The judge began to sing the Shakespearian song. "What is she? That all her swains commend her?"

The weak, dusty voice was cheerful. As Sylvia came up to the bed, she saw the judge's death in Han's serene gaze. The sick man was as gray as before, but not like clay. More like clay turning to powder. Clay dust, an ancient land between two rivers where history began.

"You're back all right. You damn women never know what you've got until you bolt. God damn right, you're back. You married the best." The judge turned his finished eyes on Han. "Your mother was in and out of our marriage like a yo-yo, but her money stayed. You're a good son, Han. A damned good son."

Han's sudden color and joyful modesty made Sylvia glance away.

"I bought another recording of E. Power Biggs, today, dad."

"What damn fool nonsense! How can you, Han?" Delighted, teasing, the judge's affectionate gaze was steady on his son. "Buried treasure, charm flower, pain killing sound waves! Undoubtedly your credulousness includes a belief in God."

Han placed the needle on the record and took a step towards the bed. The sound of the universe was in the silence of the first groove as Han, gracefully martial, quietly shining, whispered: "There's bound to be – got to be something."

Sylvia rushed down the stairs, the liquor bottle in the dark of the kitchen cupboard her passionate goal. The yearning and despair engendered by the scene upstairs possessed her with frightening strength. She remained drinking in the kitchen until Doc eventually stepped through the cellar door.

Enchanted, Sylvia jumped down from the kitchen counter and cordially presented him with the bottle of whiskey.

"No pain, dear Netop!" Pressing it to her lips when Doc handed it back, she followed him into the dining room, then held the door as he delicately angled the last Hitchcock chair through the narrow space. The fascination of the now empty room held her too long, for when she turned back to the kitchen, Doc had disappeared.

One hand on the banister, the other holding the chair, Doc was near the bottom of the cellar stairs. On the last step he picked a flashlight off a shelf. Shivering, Sylvia gave a cheer as he held the strong beam on a battered blue door. The furnace clicked on as she passed. As Doc carefully fitted the antique into the tunnel, Sylvia swallowed the last inch of whiskey and felt her body turn blond and military. She was the handsome soldier doll.

As he pushed ahead, Doc blocked the light that guided him. Sylvia gripped his tunic and placed her feet squeamishly in the dark. The tunnel floor was soft and moist. A medicinal smell puffed up her nostrils as Doc's shoulders scraped both walls. From roots or spider webs, the continual tickle of her head and temples kept her free hand passing over her hair. She began to pant although she was aware of no unusual exertion.

"Lift your feet now," Doc cautioned as he took a long step and straightened up. Sylvia jumped over a rotting door and could hardly breathe for excitement. A basket of laundry blocked the stairs. Its bottom rasped on the concrete floor as Doc nudged it with his foot. The smell of this dry, clean underground place filled her with a trembling thankfulness.

"You've brought through the last piece," she murmured. "They're the gypsies now." He disappeared and Sylvia stood up in Alison's kitchen, looking around her. The whiskey had softened her reasoning, the passage had brought her back. Tottering a little, she turned to the laundry basket. Soon the clothes were washing. Watching them snapped back and forth by the metal arms of the old machine, Sylvia fitted a word to the sound.

"Back, back, back," she exulted. "I'm back."

She adored the old zinc sink and the clothes wringer bolted to one edge. The shriek of the handle as she pushed it sharpened her excitement. That ironing board and the large, wicker basket filled with clothes to be pressed! Sylvia tugged out a pair of blue jeans and a navy-blue jersey. Ironing, the smell of the hot cotton increased her joy to pain. Her chest was too small for such feeling. Her stomach blazed.

At first it seemed that the jeans were far too narrow to stretch across her hips. Oh, no! She was adamant! When the zipper was up and finally locked, Sylvia gazed down at her brutally sheathed stomach and bottom with intense, martial pride.

The kitchen was cozy with the bulk of furniture. Edging through, Sylvia recognized the dining room table from across the way.

"Carrying those table sections one at a time – it must have taken forever. Forever!" She smiled at Doc.

"You're late. Peter was sick today. The house is a wreck!"

"Better late than never." Sylvia touched Doc's busy hand and climbed to the pantry.

Holy hell! Alison would kill if she saw this! Dirty pots and dishes crowded the counters and choked the sink. Only the white walls of the narrow pantry met the standard of cleanliness Alison imposed on the house. As though decrying the disgusting mess, every drawer hung open, even the fridge, for crying out loud!

"Thank you, my dear." Sylvia smiled broadly as a vodka bottle presented itself from behind the milk cartons. The curve and glow of the smoky glass was graciousness itself. "I agree with you. Work like a peasant, drink like one. Work, work, work. Drink, drink, drink." She put back the milk cartons and closed the refrigerator door, vodka in hand. To be sure it was closed, she leaned for a moment, then closed all the drawers and cupboards in the pantry.

The boys' bedroom, squalor and order dividing the space, clearly showed the character of two brothers. Candy bar wrappers, sexy magazines, gray underwear, and a soda bottle jammed with cigarette butts comprised the litter surrounding Freddy's bed. That child devoured sweets by the ton and the terrible trash he read had made him prurient in spite of Alison's virtuous example. He insulted his mother every turn of the way and was constantly inciting his brother to join his persecution. But Peter worshipped his mother and did his homework.

Look now: The boys had opened the leaves of a lovely maple table that Doc had just refinished and were both working in the living room. In his bathrobe, Peter's face was flushed, his eyes swollen.

"How'd she get into your jeans! Freddy? She's so drunk."

"Shut up, Peter." Freddy was predictably rude.

'Why do you have on Freddy's jeans?"

Sylvia admired the crisp line of her legs. "I look good in jeans. I'm going to be the first partner on Wall Street who wears jeans to the office." She sank down on the couch to enjoy Peter's merriment.

"My mother should have let me wear jeans to the school dances. Guys would have danced with me. I would have been popular."

Then she spotted Alison's black check book on the table. "What are you doing with that? Your mother's check book? My god, she'll kill you, Peter. What are you doing with it?"

"Your stomach's hanging out! Look at it!" Peter jumped up. "Why aren't you cleaning like you always do? Why aren't you washing the dishes? Go on, dopey. Go clean the pantry."

"What a shit you are, Peter," Freddy shouted as his brother left the room. "You're a real shit! No, Sylvia. No housework tonight."

Freddy dragged a chair beside his at the maple table. Holding it for her, he bowed and smiled. "Are you too bombed to add and subtract?"

"Not if I can have a drink."

"Hold on." Freddy bounded away.

"You look adorable," Sylvia whispered to her knees. Those school dances had not been pleasant. And no, she hadn't been attractive. A great stone of shyness and earnest hope. The great mass of the normal wore these pants of martial blue. Women and men, boys and girls. And now, she did.

"I belong!" Her voice rang off the descending vodka bottle.

"Dear Freddy! What a wonderful surprise."

Incredulous but agreeable, the boy sat down beside her and picked up his pen. "You don't remember one minute to the next."

"Certainly, I do. Vodka's so pretty, don't you think?"

"Peter's sorry he told you to clean the kitchen."

"Did he mistake me for the cleaning woman?"

"So, wait – tell me what Peter was wearing."

"When?"

"You're very drunk." His friendly face was close to hers. "What's five and seven?"

"Twelve." She threw out her hand. "See how sober I am?"

"Mother goes into a coma when she drinks a lot."

Freddy wrote a check to the neighborhood butcher for $338.12. "You erase yourself. You lead a double life and you don't know it."

"How could I know it if I don't know it?" She poked him. "How cogent."

Freddy opened the telephone bill and threw it away with a shrug. Watching him open his mother's mail, Sylvia gently expressed her anxiety concerning this unlawful activity. She could not bear for him the consequences of his mother's wrath.

Writing out another check, Freddy explained that whenever he put money in his mother's account, he was supposed to go through the bills. Today, running from school, he'd deposited a thousand dollars before the bank closed.

"I'm not stealing!" He laughed at her alarm. "I can tell you because you won't remember. I deal drugs, mostly coke. I work for this kid in school. He's so busy with heroin that he makes a fortune. He let me take over the cocaine. I don't do badly – enough to run this place. Enough to pay for Peter's snotty private school. God, does he hate to hear me remind him of that. It kills him!"

"Madison Liquor," he read. "€375.00. The week before, it was in the four hundreds. Okay." Freddy stacked the addressed envelopes and slipped the pen into the checkbook's spiral binding. "Now mother just has to sign these, and I can relax for another month."

"You're so chipper," Sylvia sorrowed. "Chipper and smart – so good of you – such sacrifice."

The lift of Freddy's eyebrows showed cheerful confusion. Barely literate, mechanically passed through an institution more prison than school, money would be the only compensation for his injured pride, and the underworld its only source. The friendly boy was doomed.

"Your mother must be so grateful!"

"Grateful?" Freddy pushed his hair clear of his amused eyes. Clearly, Sylvia was out of her skull. The night they'd snuck into this house, having driven in from Pleasantville, Alison had announced to her sons that if they didn't come up with some money she'd be forced to pick up men on the streets.

"She's great," Sylvia whispered. "The core of your mother is self-sacrifice."

"Bullshit, Sylvia! Mother watches soap operas all day in bed and drinks all night. Look how fat she's gotten."

"She's not fat."

"She's no good."

Suddenly frightened of Freddy's expression, Sylvia glanced at the door. Alison stood there, a ruddy bulk. The strained wool of her pink bathrobe was clasped at the front by a row of small buttons. Sylvia winced at the terrific tension of the buttons' clasp.

Freddy rose from the table and dropped his head as Alison took hold of his shoulders and began her tragic litany. She had never been happy. No one had ever made her happy. From the beginning of her life to this present dismal moment, no one had ever given her a moment of happiness.

Freddy drooped in her grip. "Can I go now?"

"Go!"

Coming to the table, Alison's breasts were distinct under her tight robe. "And you, you're another deserter." She tossed back the vodka Sylvia poured out and gestured for another.

"Jamming yourself into Freddy's jeans. Your masochism is ludicrous these days - and ugly!"

Wincing with disgust, Alison sat down before the checkbook. "If I find out that Freddy was paying bills in front of you and you didn't check his arithmetic ... " Alison's chest expanded with threat and a button popped off, rolling beneath the table. "Slip under and get it, please," she demanded.

On her hands and knees under the table, careful not to touch Alison's elegant feet, Sylvia skimmed the thick rug with both hands. When had the promise of love ever wrapped her so close?

Looking up from under the table, Sylvia saw Freddy standing calmly by his mother's chair.

"What are you buying, you little grafter?" She snapped.

"Oh, god!" She started to rant. If Freddy wasn't cheating her, then the stores were! The liquor bill was outrageously out of line and the nerve of the electric company! A month-long vigil was what that bill implied, night and day, every lamp and light in the house ablaze.

"One, two, three, four. Four lamps in this tiny room – all on! Even so – *you* can't find the button! Time's up, Sylvia."

Alison's nasty knock on the table top deepened Sylvia's gloom. She would never find it. The futility of her softly brushing hands was a nightmare.

"Where is Sylvia?" Freddy asked.

"She's looking for my button."

Freddy's upside-down face and thick hair came into view.

"Sylvia!" Crouching, he held out his hand. "You don't have to do that. Come out from there! Come on!"

"Bitches out of my way! Shitting, pissing, farting bitches, out of my way." The voice of the witch who'd trampled her, shrieking with hatred rang in Sylvia's head. Had that been Alison too?

As she stood up, she saw a fat untidy woman walking briskly away. Swept to a desolate freedom, Sylvia called out "Goodbye".

Freddy insisted on walking her back through the yard. The feeling of his hand in hers recalled his sneakers. Freddy and his sneakers were imperturbable.

"Why is it so frightening to feel like nothing?" She squeezed Freddy's hand. "Why isn't it peaceful?"

He pointed to their shadows, the two thick cubes across the fish pool. "You just think you're nothing."

Sylvia studied her shadow. No more or less than any other object in the yard, her body blocked the rays of moonlight.

"I just think I'm nothing." No matter what she thought,

she was something, just like everyone in the world until death's explosion.

"I'm not different," Sylvia stoutly declared, instantly doubtful. The head of her shadow was at the top of the kitchen steps. Bending crisply as she climbed, it flowed over Freddy and the open door. "I'm not different," she affirmed, grabbing the counter.

"Not in any bad way." Freddy followed her eyes as she looked up to the cupboard. "Except you drink too much."

"I do my work," she whispered. "I always get up and go to work."

"Sylvia, you look so frightened. Don't have a drink." He dashed out a chair. "Sit down. Just sit right here and I'll make you cocoa. If I go get a blanket, will you promise not to get the bottle down?"

"Okay." Sylvia watched the clock for comfort. Freddy was back in a few minutes, a fur coat slung over his arm.

"Oh, thank you!" Sylvia said, pulling the coat around her in an agony of cold. After a moment, she added, "You don't squeeze blood into a dead body."

"What do you mean?"

"I won't be drinking anymore."

Sipping cocoa, shaking hard, Sylvia accepted Freddy's skepticism without resentment.

"I'm sick now. The liquor's no use." Avidly, she sipped the cocoa. "This is so good."

Huddling down inside the fur collar, she couldn't stop sucking the hot, sweet, chocolate.

"How did Doc miss the coat?"

"Must be fake."

"I love it. I love you, Freddy. Holy hell," she crooned. "I'm really, really sick…"

CHAPTER 23

Sylvia looked so fragile now. She looked as though a punch could crush her skull. Freddy leaned against the stove while Han put the creamed chicken he'd carried upstairs to Sylvia back in the double boiler.

"It's weird, man! Same time, same station, day after day. Maybe Sylvia's a creature from outer space. Maybe they didn't mean for her to be here for so long and they've put her on repeat."

Sylvia hadn't been drinking since the night she came down with the flu, but for three nights in a row she'd gone through the same routine.

"She's like an actress playing a part."

"I wish she was," Freddy said. "I wish she'd stop coming through that door in that ratty fur coat moaning that she's cold. Freddy hunched over his folded arms, shambling to the table and mimicking Sylvia's plaintive voice. "'Why am I freezing? Why am I so weak?'", "'I could hardly get down the stairs. I'm trembling like a leaf. I can't help Alison tonight. I've got to back to bed. I can't go back to bed. Alison's already so tired, she's going to get sick.'"

Then Freddy looked guiltily at the opening door. As Sylvia shambled to the table, hunched and slow in the large fur coat, Freddy mouthed her words exactly. Why was she freezing, why was she so weak? She could hardly get down the stairs.

"She's already so tired. She's going to get sick!" Sylvia and Freddy said together.

"Stop that!"

"*You* stop it!" Freddy topped her indignation. "Mother can clean the house herself. You don't have to help her anymore."

"Someone has to help her when she's so exhausted. Cleaning up your damned mess day after day – you parasite!" Sylvia pointed at Freddy then tucked her trembling hand back under her arm.

"Sylvia, you're full of shit. Mother's the bum. She doesn't pick up men. She drinks all night. She doesn't pick up men, Sylvia. She boozes and sleeps, boozes and sleeps and I pay all the bills. You can't be surprised. You can't be frightened!" When there was no response, guiltily he shouted at her.

"You heard the same thing last night and the night before."

The door to the yard was stuck. Whispering to herself, groaning, Sylvia tugged the knob, then rattled it pathetically. Glancing at her, Han turned to the dishes in the sink.

"Want to see what you looked like that night when mother sent you under the table to get her button?" Freddy ducked under the table and crouched. "Look, Sylvia. Take a look!"

"You damned brat!" Sylvia whispered. "I didn't look like that! I couldn't have because I didn't feel that way. I know how I felt when I was looking for the button. You're such a brat!"

To hide her eyes from Freddy as she stumbled to the stairs, Sylvia's face, for a moment, was turned to Han. The shame he saw passed like lightning through his heart.

"Can I have some cocoa, too?" Again Freddy was crowding him at the stove. "Sylvia acts as though we're stupid. It's like she's trying to brainwash us. Like she's going drum into us that mother's a noble woman if it takes ten years. Don't you hate that?"

"What if her amnesia is real?"

"Liquor makes her puke these days. So how could she still be not remembering? I don't get it."

"Neither do I."

"Look, dad." Freddy pulled a roll of quarters out of his pocket. He was going down to the pizza parlor to play the electronic games.

"Only you can afford that hemorrhage of cash night after night," laughed Han.

"I'm paying." Eager eyes showed in the fling of his bangs. "You're getting good at Monte Carlo. Tonight, you can play it as much as you want. Are you coming?"

"I want to. I will later if I can."

"You don't want to."

"I do!"

Freddy brightened then looked grave. "Sylvia's really nice. I'm glad she's stopped drinking. Most of the time she's not bats in the belfry. Most of the time she's great!" At the door Freddy shook his head in wonderment.

"Mother doesn't pick up men to support the household. I know Sylvia knows that."

Han slowly climbed, hating the electronic world that was about to absorb his son, that left him alone with fear and confusion.

As always, when Han came into the third-floor room, he was met with Sylvia's politely expressed fear that her heart was stopping, but the nightly argument with Freddy was never mentioned.

"I hate to bother you, I know you're so busy with your father, but I can feel my heart slowing down again. This time I'm certain, it's on its last run. I can't feel it, Han." Shifting to the wall, Sylvia made room for him on the bed. "I must be dying." She clung to his arm as he pressed his palm to her breast.

"Strong and slow, just like always."

"Slow?" She quavered.

Han pressed his palm against her brow and said as he always did that a slow heart beat was the most cheerful of news to a doctor, the sign of a muscle strengthened and enlarged from vigorous use.

"Hey, athlete," he whispered, "when are you going back on the court?"

"Court?" Tears filled up her eyes. "I can't even get myself

across the yard. Oh, Han! All her life she's hung on, hung on, fighting envy and despair. When she saw you on the street, she was so shocked! She was coughing and sweating, then she asked me to have a drink with her. She was terrific. So strong!"

Waiting it through, his face flushed at her insane grief, suddenly he remembered commuting home to Pleasantville.

"You don't feel you're being repetitive, do you? Neither did I." Han felt they were both running out of a gloomy forest. "For years I was just like you. Every afternoon I was in love and every night half dead with disappointment. In the morning, oblivion, just like you. I couldn't give up what I thought Alison was. I couldn't give up being in love."

Sylvia's steady, polite attention neither flickered nor flared. "I'm not in love with Alison, Han."

"I agree. You're in love with who you thought Alison was."

"You're theory happy. You've got to get back downtown. I do have an ideal about Alison, but it's to do with friendship, not love."

"Come off it, Sylvia!" He laughed. "We've both been through hell."

She sat up against the headboard and gazed at him as though it might be time to call for help. "I'm sorry to be so blank, Han, but I really don't know what you're talking about."

"Come on, Sylvia. We've both been in love with Alison. Forget your career for once. I'm talking about deep things."

"You seem to be announcing in a shout that I'm a lesbian. I find that alarming."

"What?" He felt he was in a film. "Your ambition makes you so stupid and vulgar. I'd throw you out if you weren't so sick."

"I am vulgar and stupid. I've never understood why you like me." Shivering, she kept trying to pull the covers to her shoulders. "But, I'm not a lesbian. I'm not that!"

Han grabbed the fur coat from the window seat and tucked it tight around her. "What does it all mean?"

"Who cares?" Sylvia hoisted to one elbow, clutching the fur collar tight around her throat. "You're on top of it all. You look down from the heights and think it's so interesting to be female, to be a lesbian. You talk like we're all in a play, and the purpose of everything and everybody is to be interesting. I don't care what anything means. I want to win."

"What's the point of winning?"

She lay back with a mean smile. "To wipe you decadent jerks off the face of the earth."

He dropped onto her, then lifted himself again so that she could free her arms. He loved her spicy smell and springy body – Damn it!! Would her gloom ever lift?

"Not off the earth, not quite off, Han," she pressed up against him, "but I'll drive you to the edge, where you can huddle in your rags and observe the interesting social upheaval."

"Alison's maid – I love you so much – isn't driving me anywhere."

"Smell the sleeve." Throwing back the coat, Sylvia drew down his head. "It's the country, a summer wind."

"The moors behind the beach to me."

"It's your smell." Sylvia kissed his cheeks and lips. Despite the chills and aches from the flu, she was feeling permeable again. "I've been in such a stew, Han, but it's over. I've got my body back."

"You even dressed like Alison. You were more homeless than I was when the tree destroyed the Pleasantville house. A rematch with your mother? Could that be Alison's draw?" His smile came and went as he looked into her bland, stubborn eyes.

"Alison and I are just friends, Han."

"If you never think about where you're going, how are you going to stop?"

"Will power!"

He hated her boarded up soul! Screw her arrogance! But when

he tried to pull away, the strength of her arms round his neck was startling.

"I drank so much, I don't remember, Han. It could be this, it could be that – don't you see? I don't have time to make sense of it yet, but I will. I promise. Later."

Han gripped her with all the force of his legs and arms. Too close to see her, he felt the heat and moisture of her breath on his face.

"Later?" He kissed her neck. "Listen, let's get married. When we win the tennis tournament at the club the plaque will read, 'Mrs. and Mr. Sylvia Stride.' No?"

Sylvia was so still. Alarmed, Han raised his head. "No?"

"No." She pulled him down. "No!"

"Mr. and Mrs. Sylvia Smith?"

"Yes!"

Han felt their beating hearts with joy. From their centers, waves raced towards each other. Through flesh and bone, two systems of spreading waves meeting, mingling, fading.

Sylvia's heart beat more slowly than his. Han matched her breathing, but still his heart kept its faster pace. The synchronization of their heartbeats – over the days, months and years – that was a worthy goal.

CHAPTER 24

"She's not Alison, dad." His hands looked enormous supporting his father's head as he lifted and turned him. His eyes were always closed these days, even when he woke to make his new cricket sound.

It was an effect of his swift deterioration that the loud whirring, which only the larynx could produce, sounded from his meager chest. While Han hunted for the oldest bruises in his arms and haunches, his father's voice was cheerful. After the second shot of charm was in his tidy, gray body, his breathing was a mild purr. When Han turned him on his side, tucked up his knees and slipped his hands under his cheek, he made no sound at all.

"Dad's a cricket trapped in a warm winter house," he'd told Sylvia. "He knows it's odd. He knows he should be dead in some frozen little hole outside – but he's here! He's here!"

Sylvia had such a pure laugh. Han loved the quick flashes of gaiety that interrupted her troubled brooding. Poor, driven girl. Han leaned his head close to his father's smooth, still face.

"Sylvia's not Alison, dad. She's a thoroughbred, a racer from the west. She doesn't spare herself. Her mother's got Indian blood in her veins but thinks like you do. She's also got the longest arm in the country. All the way across from the Pacific she's whipping her little thoroughbred, whipping her, whipping her. That was Sylvia on the tennis court, dad, not Alison. The last time you played tennis, we beat you. We won!"

"I'm in love and I'm sticking it out because soon Sylvia's ferocious mother is going to look just like you."

Touching his hair, kissing his brow, just what did his father look like now?

A pot. An ancient pot. The sort of pot in which the old woman of the myths keeps the winds. Now almost empty. Han slipped onto his knees and lowered his face until his father's breath was the faintest pressure on his cheek. He had been swept all his life by his father's force. Where had that ferocious wind come from? Where had it gone?

Han stood. He turned out the lamps in each corner and came back to the bed. Tucked and folded, the form so obedient to his arranging was his father. Was he dead? A tiny breath warmed his fingers. Swept by the wind to be swept again, but not quite yet.

"You'll travel light, dad, too light to damage."

THE END

AUTHOR JOAN HAWKINS

Joan Hawkins was born in Cambridge, Massachusetts. She attended Bennington College and New York University. She lived most of her life in Manhattan, where she practised psychotherapy.

Her debut novel, *Underwater*, was published by GP Putnam in 1974. The book was critically acclaimed, challenging traditional gender roles and exploring controversial issues of the day. A second edition of *Underwater* was published on its fortieth anniversary by Landon Books in 2014.

The author's second novel, *Bailey* (2012), explores themes of addiction and childhood trauma. *Trespass* (2013), is a fascinating portrait of a moribund, spirited woman living joyously to the end. Joan's fifth work, *Family Money*, was published by 451 Editions in 2022 along with the electronic edition of *Underwater*.

For more, see: www.JoanHawkins.net